MW01156307

BEST
LESBIAN
EROTICA
2013

BEST
LESBIAN
EROTICA
2013

Edited by

KATHLEEN WARNOCK

Selected and Introduced by

JEWELLE GOMEZ

CLEiS
PRESS

Published in the United States by Cleis Press Inc., 2246 Sixth Street, Berkeley, California 94710.

Printed in the United States.
Cover design: Scott Idleman/Blink
Cover photograph: Phyllis Christopher
Text design: Frank Wiedemann
First Edition.
10 9 8 7 6 5 4 3 2 1

Trade paper ISBN: 978-1-57344-896-3
E-book ISBN: 978-1-57344-912-0

"Pool Party," by Zoe Amos, was published as an ebook on Amazon Kindle (2011); "Daffodils," by Sally Bellerose, was published in *Pillowtalk* (Alyson, 1998) and *Ripe Fruit* (Cleis Press, 2002); "Lessons for Leona," by Tenille Brown, was published on Oysters & Chocolate (2011); "Stella Loves Bella," by V. C. Clark, was published on Oysters & Chocolate (2008); "Winner Take All," by Andrea Dale, was published in *The Harder She Comes* (Cleis Press, 2012); "Underskirts," by Kirsty Logan, was published in *The Winners Bridport Prize 2010* (Redcliffe Press, 2011); "La Caída," by Anna Meadows, was published in *Girls Who Bite* (Cleis Press, 2011); a flash fiction version of "The Invitation," by Maggie Veness, titled "Letter Under the Door," was published in *In My Bed* magazine (2010); "Crave," by Fiona Zedde, was published as "Dreamtime" in *Best Lesbian Romance 2007* (Cleis Press, 2007).

CONTENTS

vii   Foreword • KATHLEEN WARNOCK

x   Introduction: On Our Backs • JEWELLE GOMEZ

1   The Invitation • MAGGIE VENESS

5   Nothing If It Fades • NIKKI ADAMS

17   Cucumbers and Cream • HELEN SANDLER

29   Anonymous • BD SWAIN

32   Woman-Time • REBECCA LYNNE FULLAN

46   Kitty and the Cat • AMELIA THORNTON

58   She Never Wears Perfume • SID MARCH

65   Amateur Night • MAGGIE MORTON

72   Crave • FIONA ZEDDE

79   Stella Loves Bella • V. C. CLARK

90   Homecoming • ANAMIKA

103 Pool Party • ZOE AMOS

116 Daffodils • SALLY BELLEROSE

124 Winner Take All • ANDREA DALE

132 Lessons for Leona • TENILLE BROWN

143 Morning Commute • PENNY GYOKERES

148 Aftermath • VALERIE ALEXANDER

157 I Have a Thing for Butches • SONYA HERZOG

168 *La Caída* • ANNA MEADOWS

183 The Horse and Hounds • RACHEL CHARMAN

196 Underskirts • KIRSTY LOGAN

207 About the Authors

212 About the Editors

FOREWORD

Santayana said, "Those who cannot remember the past are condemned to repeat it." I would like to add that those who *do* remember it will come up with a great guest judge for *Best Lesbian Erotica*.

Among her many smart decisions, Tristan Taormino, the founder of this series, asked Jewelle Gomez to edit the 1997 volume. It was the second year of *Best Lesbian Erotica*, and getting Jewelle to select the stories was a major step in the growth and visibility of the book and the genre. This year, when we were discussing possible guest judges, I asked the folks at Cleis: "Could we do repeats?"

I'd had a chance to meet and work with Jewelle earlier in the year, when TOSOS (the LGBT theater company in New York, of which I am a proud member) produced a staged reading of her new play, *Waiting for Giovanni*. It's a beautiful and challenging piece about James Baldwin, one of our great American writers, by an artist whose own voice is more powerful than ever. So we asked Jewelle to select this year's stories and were thrilled when she said yes.

In the fifteen years since Jewelle last worked with *Best Lesbian Erotica*, the genre has become a mighty one, evolving into a full-voiced maturity, with a loyal audience, and writers whose work stands with the best in any genre. I was proud to pass the finalists on, and wondered which she'd choose: which writers would have their first story published, which of the emerging ones would keep blossoming, which grown artists would thrill us with a masterful tale.

One of the most important things we do as artists, one of our obligations, is to make it possible for others to tell their stories. So each spring when I begin to sort through hundreds of stories, I look and listen hard for the ones that are most necessary. What we do: naming and owning our desires, our loves, our fears, our deepest secrets, is essential. Saying, "No, I am HERE, this is who I am," is crucial to living when scared, angry people try to erase us, deny us, legislate us out of existence, make us second-class citizens, third-class...nothing.

In Jewelle's beautiful play about James Baldwin, the artist is pressured not to publish *Giovanni's Room*: a book about two men, white men, who love each other. His editor begs him to consider another topic; many of his fellow African American writers think he should be writing about their struggle to achieve equality. And finally, Baldwin picks up his papers from the floor and says:

> ...Still, I can do no more than bind my own wounds and remind them that not accepting love is where the end begins. Each book is my way of wringing life from death. And this story is one I...need...to tell and he is the one I wish to tell it. Unknown. Loving with the certainty of the tides.
>
> And my life, my needs, my questions are my own

to be examined by me...read by many. But judgment? In the beginning was the word...words made from the breath of life. It is the same breath whether we are singing a praise song or taking in the scent of our beloved who lies naked beside us. No matter how fierce my need may be; no matter how loud the sound of those who turn away—I am always me...inside *here*, looking out. Bearing witness. Preaching the word.

Kathleen Warnock
New York City

INTRODUCTION: ON OUR BACKS

Jewelle Gomez

Back in 1984, when I was asked to submit an erotic story to the magazine *On Our Backs*, I'd never written one before. Of course, I had fantasies like most people (I was, after all, raised Catholic!); but as for writing them down—it never occurred to me. As a lesbian feminist of color I wasn't against erotic literature; I just wasn't sure how one constructed a juicy story that wasn't based on exploitation. But I was already formulating the ideas for my vampire novel, a story told through a feminist lens, so I had begun thinking about how to tackle a traditionally exploitative genre without traveling down the easy road of tradition. So I figured I might as well give erotica a go, too. The challenge of finding the "sweet spot" while creating engaging, multidimensional women who are not taking advantage of each other (unless that was mutual) was a challenge I enjoyed.

The other part of wanting to write the story was a response to a call to action by the Feminist Anti-Censorship Taskforce

(FACT) which, in the 1980s, was providing a sex-positive political alternative to the very loud voices of conservative, antiporn activists. Women's relationship to sexuality was and remains a complex territory. No matter how hip and powerful we feel, women have been and continue to be seen as the sexual receptacles for men. Male-produced images in popular culture still define us so narrowly it would be impossible for an extraterrestrial being landing on earth to actually recognize a female unless the being had landed in the offices of a fashion magazine where the women are dress-size 0, wear six-inch heels, and all look white, even when they have brown skin. Female images in popular media are crafted to pique the desire of middle-aged white men. And any women that seem to deviate from that are quickly slapped down—see "journalists'" comments about Kate Winslet or Kelly Clarkson being "fat." Notice how few African American women with dark skin or Asian American women appear on magazine covers or on television series. This affects how we treat ourselves and our desire.

Mainstream pornography simply follows mainstream commercial images to their logical conclusion: women are not people…we're *soylent green*. That is—like the eponymous movie—we are a packaged edible, human commodity to be used, abused and discarded at the whim of male consumers. The famous picture that antiporn activists used most often was that of a porn magazine cover in which women were being fed into a meat grinder, legs and high heels the only remaining indication that we were humans. There is no question that these images cause damage. But I'd venture to say that numerically speaking, many more people have their ideas about women shaped by going to auto shows; watching the Kardashians, the Dallas Cowboy Cheerleaders and children's beauty pageants; all of the above being alarming cases where women contribute to their own objectification or that of their children, usually without a thought about the pornographic quality of their acts. All of it supports the idea that women are disposable and interchangeable items as easily killed off as changing the tires on your truck.

That said, it is just as dangerous for women to tamp down our sexuality in response to exploitation, and that is what conservative lesbian feminists of the '80s were insisting on. Should we don the not-so-gay apparel of the cloister? Never enjoy our fantasies? Never experience orgasm because it frightens the horses? When President Ronald Reagan sent Attorney General Edwin Meese on a fact-finding mission, Meese traveled the country, holding meetings, trying to convince local municipalities to shut down "porn" operations. The commission engaged "experts" who emphatically declared that if we didn't fight this scourge we were Nazis.

A group of us—mostly lesbian—activists went to a courthouse hearing of the commission in New York City, smuggling in signs that said CENSORED and we whipped them out at one point, and sat quietly so it would look really bad if they tried to drag us away. The resulting Commission report didn't tell us anything we didn't already know, and told us a lot that was totally untrue. The result of the Commission, its report and the so called "porn wars" was not a lessening in the profits of porn magazines or increase in the recognition of responsible human beings, but rather the clamping down on and sometimes ban of gay and lesbian literature (erotic and not) crossing borders.

I know what it's like to have female sexuality abused. African women were used by slave masters as if they were one of the mules on the plantation; Native women were raped and eviscerated for sport; and every day in the news we see the reports of only a fraction of the rapes and domestic beatings that occur. But women do have a right to sexual expression that we control and we have to be suspicious of any male authority attempting to maintain control over our bodies, whether it's about what we wear in public, what we do in bed or what we do or do not carry in our wombs: these things are connected.

It's no accident that lesbians have been at the forefront of that activism trying to hold on to our right to be sexually active and exploratory. We have been declared outlaws for our sexual desire; or worse, told that we (as women) didn't have any real desire. One of the last things I did before I left New York City was participate in a collective that created a one-day conference (in 1992) called Lesbians Undoing Sexual Taboos—LUST. It featured panels, readings, demonstrations (a lot of women found Annie Sprinkle's G-spot that day), and it culminated in a dance at the Clit Club complete with a back room for experimentation. I am forever in debt to the women who engaged me in FACT and LUST for expanding my understanding of the significance of desire in our political lives.

I tell this history not to be downbeat, but to indicate how important these stories in this anthology are and celebrate them! I tell the history so that we don't forget how easily and self-righteously some would take away our right to speak these stories out loud; and so that the younger writers included in this anthology know they are part of a heroic tradition. Women and lesbians are not having an easy passage into liberation and there are those who still believe our bodies are their own personal colonies; to paraphrase Maya Angelou… "and still we rise."

The variety of stories here will testify to the breadth and variety of lesbian desire and the triumph of freedom of expression. Each one is my favorite, of course, because they all elicit the sense of anticipation or surprise or fun and the desire that makes life worth living. No one really knows what raises our blood pressure, engorges our sexual organs and gets our hearts pumping;

it's a complexity of biology, history and imagination. But each of these authors has created a singular landscape in which she has expert control over the facets of desire for her characters and succeeds in getting the juices flowing, figuratively and literally. Whether you're listening carefully for the soft, tantalizing rustle of voluminous gowns in the sensual treasure "Underskirts," by Kirsty Logan, or you're moving with the hard-driving need of "Anonymous," by BD Swain, you'll find the core elements of erotica that are key to our lives as lesbians. These are elements we don't give up easily even in the face of repression or censorship. On our backs we are not helpless like the crab or turtle; we are open and moist, ready for fulfillment. At the same time we're ready to spring up to show the power of our desire. As Audre Lorde said, "Our visions begin with our desires."

THE INVITATION

Maggie Veness

Dear Ella,

This is Stevie from two doors down. Sorry about leaving this under your door, but I was wondering, would you like to go out for coffee with me?

(You've been on my mind since last month when we spoke briefly at that carnival. At the time you had a small child asleep on your shoulder and I introduced myself while that worn calliope recording was crackling away in the background—told you I was sure we both lived here on the second floor at 151 Lincoln, me in Number 9. You smiled, said we'd passed each other on the stairs a few times, that you were in Number 7. That's when I saw it...

I caught that split second when your shiny, green eyes swept from my lips to my flat chest, brushed down over my thighs, then flicked back to my face. That glance was like hearing the first few words of a tantalizing secret—whispered once, then locked away—and was so exciting that ever since then I've fantasized about feeling your amazing body surrender to my hungry hands and mouth. I think about you and get this long, slow pulse in my temples. It slides down my spine like a warm tongue, then moves to my belly and continues to grow until desire collides with opportunity—and my impatient fingers carry out an orgasmic exorcism.)

Do you have a favorite café? I'm happy to take you anywhere you like.

(I saw you yesterday from my kitchen window, chatting with neighbors down in the leafy courtyard. You looked pretty in that sky-blue satin blouse and denim skirt. I noticed the careful way you folded your washing as you talked, meeting corners neatly together, flicking and smoothing everything down with your slender, pointy fingers. I also noticed how the lean tendons in your arms flexed when you gathered that overflowing cane basket against your streamlined body.)

And, if you enjoyed our coffee date, would you consider having dinner with me?

(I also saw you last Saturday afternoon, when I took a shortcut home through Brayford Park after work. You were sitting on a wooden bench watching your son play, and I must confess to resting awhile in the shade of a nearby fig tree. After a few minutes you wandered down to join him. I saw your cheeks color and your eyes flash when you ran fast and low to the ground. You guys were having so much fun tumbling and rolling about together, in fact, just hearing all the squealing and laughter made me feel happy. By the time the chasing games were over and you headed home, there were a few wild, red curls fused to your damp forehead.

I want to play too, Ella. I want to take you by the wrists, swing you around and around and watch your aerodynamic body skim and soar. I want to see your skin blush pink as your excitement grows. I want to make you squeal.

After you'd disappeared from view I sat on the same park bench and imagined you next to me, radiating your own brand of pure sunburst energy, your smooth, bare legs *so* wide apart...*so* open to experiment. I swear I felt the warmth of your afterglow.)

Then, if dinner went well, would you come away with me for a weekend?

(I could drive you to the coast; take you up to my favorite lookout. We could hold hands and lean way out above the windy cliff face; breathe in the salt air while the sea breaks over the pebbled beach way below. If you wanted to, you could follow me along the overgrown track to this special place I know—a secluded, flat-roofed Spanish bungalow with lime-washed walls and two metal sunrays sitting like eyebrows over the small front windows.

In my favorite fantasy I lock the door behind us, tenderly kiss your mouth and begin to slowly undress you. After undoing the tiny buttons on your blue satin blouse, I slip my palms beneath the fabric and slide it off your strong shoulders. I gently bite your neck, stroke the rippling curve of your ribs, draw out your dark nipples and suck four of your fingers into my mouth. Eventually, I drag your skirt and panties to the floor.

After leading you to the low bed, I ease you down onto fresh cotton sheets, and use my tongue to wash your salty body. I shuck your oyster and hold your pearl between my lips until I hear you growl with pleasure, then turn my hand into a snake and wriggle inside you 'til the veins in your long neck protrude and your eyes roll back. Frantic by now, I scissor my legs and slide back and forth against your heat until we both arch and jerk and scream with ecstasy.

We fall asleep like that, with our warm, pivoted sex pressed together, our glistening fur tangled into one perfectly woven female fabric.)

Sorry, Ella. I'm getting ahead of myself suggesting dinners and weekends away. Let's start again. Will you join me for coffee? I promise it'll be fun.

(Tonight, after you've retreated to the privacy of your bedroom, know that I'll be nearby in Number 9 imagining those tapered fingers drawing circles between your wet thighs as you consider my invitation. And if my hunch is right and you find my invitation appealing, please withdraw those sweet-tasting fingers and write me your reply. Then, if you should find sleep eludes you, just take that note and tiptoe along our dim, quiet corridor and push it underneath my door—straight into my eager, wet fingers.)

I look forward to hearing back from you soon.

Stevie

P.S. A note under my door would be just fine.

NOTHING IF IT FADES

Nikki Adams

I dabbed the blood from his left shoulder blade, checked for gaps and light spots, then started switching out the three point for a single. "Gonna start the fines now. You doing all right, Dylan?"

"Uh-huh, I'm good."

I cast a quick look around. Larry was in his groove, buzzing away on a walk-in I hadn't seen before. The high school kid was somewhere up front, rearranging the flash, cleaning up or just plain goofing off. I leaned a little closer. "Sweetie, you look like you lost more weight. Sure you're okay?"

Dylan shifted his head just enough for me to glimpse the curve of an eye. He swallowed. "I'm okay." A slight pull came to the corner of his mouth. "They say I've still got some sand in the glass, so don't you worry!" I kissed the gold and yellow koi that perpetually swam down his other shoulder, then turned back to my gun. "Are you hitting on me again?"

"Yea, right! You just keep dreaming, Bucko!"

"Tell me something, CJ? Have you joined the club yet?"

Everyone called me CJ—even the sign out front said so, leaving many to approach the door before realizing the nature of my little business. Some would wander in then later come back as customers. The first months in my two-story house and business had been slow, but word soon got around. Things picked up and I hired Larry, who, good in his own right, brought even more business. I was one of only a few female ink-slingers in the state who ran her own shop. Some said I was the best. That always struck me as kind of funny, since I thought I was just meticulous—perhaps obsessively so.

"Which club is that? You're gonna have to be a little more specific."

"The 'More Than One Tat' club," Dylan said with a smile.

"The one I have is just fine."

"Oh, come on! What kind of inker only has one tattoo?"

"My kind," I answered. "I'm the artist, not the canvas." I loaded the needle and buzzed off the excess.

"Uh-huh. So, when are you gonna let me see it?"

"Fuck you," I said, pushing him forward a little. "How many times you gonna ask me that? Now get comfy, and quit moving." He snickered. I started on the whiskers of his second koi—this one to be a wealth of dazzling blues to offset the other. I wondered if, perhaps, he were entrusting them to carry him downstream—that part of him they were able to move—to a pond somewhere beyond the fear that had become his life.

Joey, the high school kid on work release, popped his head in. "CJ? There's someone out front who wants a tat. He's asking for you."

"Did you tell him I'm booked solid for two months?"

"Yea, but he seems kinda particular about it."

I blinked a few times. "How you doing, Dylan? Can you hang?"

"I'm good either way."

"I'll be out in ten minutes." Joey moved off and I went back to the design on Dylan's shoulder, soon losing myself in the fine lines of the scales. Pause, dab, reload and resume—the gentle curves, one after another, upon another, over and over. During one such pause, I heard Dylan whisper back to me.

"Have you talked to Vi?"

My world shifted, insides trembling upon that solitary word.

Vi…

Violet.

"Shouldn't be too difficult. Who would you like to do it?"

Her long black hair rested against her shoulders as she turned her head, green eyes looking first down the hall, then back to me. "I think I'd rather…I'd prefer your hands, if that's all right with you? I'm sorry, I—I know it's getting late, but I'd really like to do it now. I don't want to chicken out again!"

She was a real looker; Larry's eyes were almost popping out as I led her back to my station. "Lower back, right? How low would you like it?"

"Very," she said in a whisper. Knowing what that meant, I cut Larry loose, promising to pay him for the extra hour and a half. "Damn," he whispered, shaking his head and smiling as he walked past me. I locked the door and flipped the sign to CLOSED. *She waited patiently as I made a copy of her drawing—a beautiful* V *in Edwardian script with some sort of flower on either side.*

"Could you bring a little vine near the sides of the V, *kind of curling around a little, with a violet on each end? Sorry I didn't draw mine very well."*

"That's okay. Well, let's see what I can find." I pulled up

some good pictures on my laptop. She watched as I worked it up on paper. "You know, I could fill in the V in light blue, and graduate the color through different shades of violet as I go down, finishing in the deepest?" I sketched it out in colored pastel pencils, blended some of them and showed her.

"Wow, that's it! That's perfect!"

"Are you sure?"

"Absolutely!"

I smiled back, worked up a final stencil and gave her the consent and care forms to sign.

"Why don't you get comfortable, and try to relax," I said. "I can change the chair into a table, if you prefer to lie down? Totally up to you."

"I can sit. I mean, you know—kinda straddle the chair."

"Okay. You'll have to hike down the jeans a little."

I sensed her green eyes following me to the copy machine, her sweet perfume teasing my senses. Shake it off, CJ, I told myself. She's not like that, and besides, she's a customer. She's putting her trust in you, so knock it off. *I went back with the working stencil and found her sitting in just her little top, panties and socks, jeans folded on the corner chair, sneakers beneath. I pulled my eyes away long enough to glance at the release and her driver's license.*

"Your name's Violet? I suppose that helped when choosing the flower!"

"Yeah, I'm kinda stuck with it."

I explained that I had to shave the area so that errant hairs, no matter how small, wouldn't be pushed back into the skin.

"So, how low can you go with it? I'd like it to be totally hidden beneath my panty line, if you could?"

"I can go as low as you want. Just so you know, it's gonna light you up. The lower you go, the more sensitive it gets."

She nodded, stood up and started easing her panties down. Then, as a ballerina might, she drew a leg almost vertically out one side, then the other. Nothing—not a solitary hair around the soft crease that vanished between her legs. Violet tossed the panties atop her jeans, smiled slightly and straddled the chair. After lathering, shaving her lower back and patting her dry, I handed her a mirror and asked her to stand. I began to locate the stencil.

"How's that?"

"Can you go lower?" I fought against the trembling of my fingertips and moved it down, then down again. She opened her legs slightly and I lowered it farther, the bottom tip of the V sitting just at the crack of her buttocks. "There," she whispered. "Right there. Is that okay, or is it too low?"

I pulled on a pair of latex gloves and, taking into account the slight shaking of my hands, chose my heavier BSI Trident over the standard, lighter Sidekick. She put a leg on either side of the chair and leaned forward, moving her ass toward me. My eyes drank in her curvaceous cheeks, the taut little hole, the soft pink lips and the hint of her tight belly where it met the towel. I set a hand on her left cheek and drew closer.

She let out a gasp as the needle hit. I bit my lip, blinked a few times, then started the slow and methodical process of outlining the stencil. She made little noises every now and then, drawing breaths against the pain. The thin black lines rose up slightly as I moved, surrounded by a slight blush. After about fifteen minutes, I had finished the outline and all the black highlights on the left side. As I gently dabbed her with a cool washcloth, she let out a combined moan and sigh.

"I'm going to start the other side now, then fill in the colors on the flowers and tendrils. We'll do the V last, okay?"

"Okay," she answered, panting slightly. "Can I...can I ask you something?"

"Of course."

She threw her black hair aside and looked over her shoulder. "What does 'CJ' stand for?"

I blinked a few times and leaned closer. "Carmen," I said softly. "My name is Carmen Jansen."

Her eyes traveled down the front of my shirt. "Beautiful," she whispered, then met my gaze again. "That's a beautiful name. Nice to meet you, Carmen."

I swallowed against a lump that had taken hold within my throat, and fleetingly worried that my chin was quivering. "Nice to meet you, Violet." She smiled and rested her head on the pillow.

After edging, highlighting and coloring both sides, I started outlining the V. Her gasps grew stronger. I moved the light closer and leaned in. As I went lower, following the letter to its bottom tip, I could smell her. She was wet. Her womanly sweetness moved into me, permeating me, making my senses tingle as they never had before. God, how I wanted her—to touch and taste her, know every inch of her soft skin. I wanted to hear her moan and scream. My mind flashed an image of her head thrown back, hands grabbing my hair and holding me against the aching delight of her clit. My breath came quicker, and I knew she could feel it landing upon her tender flesh.

Finishing the outline, I ripped open a sterile three-point needle. She watched over her shoulder, mouth slightly open as I mixed a variety of blue and purple shades in the dipping tray.

By the time I neared filling in the letter, her gasps had turned to moans. Violet's face, pressed sideways against the pillow by the arching of her back, was covered with a scattering of hair and tiny beads of sweat. Her left hand was atop mine as I held her buttocks apart. Her right was tucked beneath her stomach. Two of her fingers were making frantic circles before disap-

*pearing. They emerged, slick and shiny, to race over her clit
again and again.*

Squirming upon my stool, I came twice just watching her.

"CJ?...CJ?"

I drew a breath. "What?"

"Sorry. Uhhh, it's been almost half an hour," Joey said. "That
guy is still waiting." I told Dylan we'd take a break and made
my way to the front.

He seemed average enough, as if anyone in this world could
be considered so, though nervous, the way squirrels are. Uncomfortable and twitchy. I apologized and asked what I could do
for him. He flipped through a book of flash on the counter. He
eventually pointed to a torn chest, ribs exposed through jagged,
bleeding flesh.

"I was thinking about something like this?"

"Just like that, as it is, or do you want something similar?
Can't afford to be vague when it comes to a tattoo." He stam-
mered and shifted for a moment. I sent Joey in back to check on
the autoclave and see if anyone wanted a bite to eat. "Okay. Tell
me exactly what you're looking for."

He blinked a few times and lifted his T-shirt. Across his
chest were four diagonal red lines, with a fifth slightly offset,
which was thinner and shorter. They looked three-dimensional
and I reached out to see how they had been drawn. He flinched
slightly. Parts of the lines had scabbed over.

"Have you been picking at these? If you keep doing that,
they'll probably end up scarring."

"I don't want them as scars," he said in a whisper. "I want
them to bleed."

While an apprentice inker, I quickly learned that people
want what they want. You don't ask them why; you just ask

them if they're sure. This guy was sure and, when I asked him a second time, he was certain again. I bit my lip and broke the unwritten rule.

"Tell me."

After a couple of false starts, he began recounting how he and his girlfriend had gotten into an argument, some sort of big scream fest involving another girl. He didn't go into specifics, though the dropping of his head and avoiding my eyes told me all there was to know. The argument got worse, he said, and she began to freak out. She cried and screamed and hit him—finally reaching the point where she gouged her fingers into his chest and raked him open. She ran from the house, squealing tires as she raced away. After twenty minutes and unable to think of anything else, he went after her.

When he came upon the scene, the rescue squad was using a pneumatic expander—trying to free her from the wreckage curled around a tree.

"Glass and metal everywhere and...I don't expect you to understand," he said. "I did that to her. I wasn't driving, but I did it all the same. And this is all I have left. She'd still be in my arms if only I'd... I'll pull the scabs off every day, if I have to. I just want you to help me to never forget. I'll be left with nothing, if it fades."

This guy would eat his own heart if he could yank it from his chest. I looked at his shirt, knowing what lay beneath, then back to him.

"I'm sorry, I can't. No, what I mean is, I won't."

He stared at me, his face a blank.

"Sorry," I said again, softly. "I'm afraid you'll have to find someone else to do it."

He stood there for a moment, then nodded. He rubbed his nose and, with eyes blank, shuffled out.

My gaze wandered down to the notebook before me. A chill lingered at the center of my spine as I drew the image from the plastic sleeve. It was in several crumpled pieces by the time it hit the bottom of the trash can.

When I got back to my station, Larry was putting the finishing touches on the walk-in and Dylan was leafing through a magazine. The smell of a cigarette lingered upon him.

"Are you kidding me? You haven't even quit smoking?"

He smiled and shrugged, favoring the shoulder I'd been working on. "What can I tell you, CJ? Can't help myself, I guess!"

"Turn around! Just turn around and assume the position!" He let out a little chuckle. *Damn it, Dylan,* I thought, reaching for a new pair of gloves.

After closing the shop, I went upstairs and popped a frozen dinner in the microwave. Twelve days had passed; twelve days since I had told her that I needed to be sure of myself. The only thing I was certain of was that I was little more than a shadow of who I'd been. I turned on the television, quietly beseeching it to numb me. I thought of that guy, wanting his cuts to be everlasting. Then memories of Vi flowed into my mind, as I knew they would.

"Hi CJ! Would you mind checking my tattoo? I can't see it very well, and I want to make sure it's healing okay."

"Why don't we go upstairs? Want some coffee?"

"Sure!"

We went up and I flipped the switch on the coffee machine. "Let's take a peek."

Violet unbuttoned her jeans and turned toward the countertop, placing both hands upon it. Looking over at me, she smiled faintly and raised one of her wonderfully arched eyebrows. I walked to her and, standing behind, eased the zipper down. Her jeans followed and, with the tips of my fingers, I gently pulled back and lowered her panties. Her flowers, vines and initial, kept moist with a thin layer of Tattoo Goo and a patch of plastic wrap, slowly revealed itself.

"Beautiful," I whispered in her ear. She turned around and, cupping my face in her hands, brought her lips to mine. Long and slow we kissed, and I soon forgot what it was to breathe.

"Come back tonight," I whispered.

She did.

I have known heat, and the few women I've been with have brought me to understand hunger. But like so many things about her, Violet's lips were different. There was yearning, but also softness and exhilaration, fear and freedom. Fingers touched necks and shoulders, as my kisses moved from her lips to the underside of her chin. One of her hands set gently upon my breast. Her fingernail traced around my nipple, then left it to strain against my T-shirt as she drew me close. Her other hand ran through my hair as I began nibbling the soft skin beneath her ear. She moaned and held me against her even tighter. Struggling through stolen breaths, we soon found our way to the bed.

Since I'm usually the aggressive one, I was surprised to find myself on my back. She crawled atop and kissed me, lightly at first, then with more passion. More urgency. Violet's tongue danced with my own as I felt her hands moving to the bottom of my T-shirt. She straddled me and, with a smile, pulled it up. As soon as my head came into view, she twisted it around my arms and held them lightly in place. Her eyes drank in my little breasts.

She kissed me once, long and deep, then quickly set upon one of my nipples. Her tongue played over it softly, sending little shivers racing down my spine. After flicking it hard a few times, *she pulled it gently upward with her teeth. Without realizing, I was arching my back to keep her mouth on me. I ached to reach out and hold her head exactly where it was, but as soon as she felt movement, her grip on my shirt tightened. Violet shifted from one breast to the other, sweetly tormenting that nipple as well. With the pulsation moving outward from my core, I ground my hips against her stomach.*

She released her grip, took off her top and bra, then leaned forward to feed me one of her breasts. Warm and soft in my hands, I played upon her nipples in much the way she had mine. Within moments, she was kissing my forehead and reaching down to rub a hand between my jean-clad legs. The wetness quickly began to move outward.

Moments later, Violet turned herself around and lowered her warm and hairless flesh within easy reach. She planted soft kisses all around my slit, licked the wetness she found there and began to flick at my bud with her tongue.

I pulled her hips slightly downward until her clit pressed against my ready and wanting mouth. We delved into each other with fingers and tongues, the trembling of hips and spasms of pressed bellies telegraphing every new sensation.

Fingers deep within each other, we licked, kissed and nibbled. Time, memories, worry—everything beyond the softness of her flesh seemed to dissolve and float away into the dim light of the room.

I urged Violet onto her back and positioned our legs. We moved and pressed against each other, quickly finding a rhythm to match the flow of desire that rose from within. With her head thrown back, she seized my hips and began to press her clit hard against my own. Several quick gasps escaped her and she pulled me in tightly. All of our lips merged. My orgasm raced to its bursting point just as a long moan escaped her. As she shuddered and shook with release, her voice shifted into a scream muffled against my neck. The grinding became gentle movement, then stillness. I pulled the sheets over us, kisses taking in the sweet sheen from each other's necks and faces.

A few nights later, we fell into each other again. And again. Daylight became something that kept us from the moon, from our true selves, though we soon conquered that as well. Weeks became three months. Sometimes she stopped in the parlor, dropping off hoagies and soup while I worked on Dylan's first koi. The semicircles of its many scales became, in my wandering mind, the curves of her body and the arc of her smile. Larry had noticed the change within my face, smiled and said nothing. Dylan picked up on it as well. "She's good for you," he whispered.

Back in the present, I turned off the television, splashed water on my face, then went and sat on the edge of the bed. The full-length antique mirror in the corner glanced back at me. It had watched us always, including the night I found myself on the brink of weeping from the melding of our souls. Her breath had fallen softly upon my neck as I held her, close as a person could without disappearing.

"I love you, Carmen."

I took the few steps toward the mirror and unbuttoned my jeans. Slowly easing down my panties, it came into view. Open and unfolded, it was an exact copy of hers, repositioned so the tendril led to the very top of my folding flesh. I moved a fingertip within myself then brought it higher. The hues of the flower, already quite vivid from daily care, glistened.

I drew a breath as the tears rose up. No longer afraid, I reached for my phone.

CUCUMBERS AND CREAM

Helen Sandler

I only went down to the bar to watch the show. I was feeling pretty chilled, rolling up there just before I expected the act to come onstage. One of the other regular MCs, Tatiana, a big brash doll of a girl in a ripped, punk T-shirt, was sitting at a table in front of the DJ booth with her manly/womanly girl-friend and cheeky-chappie boyfriend. The entwined group was like an ad for the genderfuck love-in that is our little club.

But when I asked, "Are you compering tonight?" Tatiana said, "No, I think you are."

I reeled away, wondering if I'd got it wrong...spinning right into the arms of the club promoter, Reno. She held me in a comforting bear hug as she asked, "You wanna host tonight?"

"I just came down to hear the band," I said.

"The band canceled, Tatiana's feeling vulnerable, Freddy wants to do tech...I can go on, but I'd love it if you'd do it."

"Oh, okay." I regrouped. "So who's on?"

"An amazing burlesque duo who are over here from Paris.

They're backstage now. Go meet them and see how they want to be introduced and we'll go on in fifteen."

"You want me to go backstage and talk to the strippers while they get changed?"

"Yes, why not?"

"Why not indeed?" I laughed, shaking my head at my good fortune.

"Just don't call them 'strippers.'"

"I should probably tell you I haven't got a pen and paper, I'm not dressed to go onstage and I'm mildly stoned. Oh, and I haven't put wax in my hair." I ran a few fingers through my gray quiff; it was fluffy instead of stiff.

"Go ask Siggy for what you need," she said, gesturing toward the DJ booth. "Wait! Lemme see what you're wearing."

I unzipped my leather jacket to reveal a hoodie and a well-worn T-shirt from the London Lesbian and Gay Film Festival with a bent signpost on the front. I didn't know what year it was from, but it wasn't recent.

"You'll do. Call it 'chilled vintage.'" She looked me in the eye. "How stoned are you?"

I knew Reno didn't approve of even the mildest of illegal substances. She had told me in the past to avoid making drug references from the stage, in case it encouraged younger people to take up the habit. But I can't take my drink, so the occasional joint is my way of unwinding.

"A bit." I crossed my eyes.

She laughed and I realized there would be no condemnations this evening. "This should be interesting. Well, you didn't plan to go on tonight and neither did they, so anything that happens will be spontaneous. And that's how we like it here!" She guffawed and I knew what she meant: that the club was all about the improvised, the *ad hoc* and the edgy—Reno took risks, so did the acts and the audience, and it generally paid off.

I tripped up to the DJ booth where our resident hipster bear, Siggy, asked me not to talk to him. "When I'm DJ-ing, I'm performing, I can't chat."

Rejected, I tripped back down to the shabby dressing room. I knocked and entered—and immediately felt welcome. Two beautiful younger women in underwear were exchanging makeup, and they smiled at me in the mirror. I tried to retain a professional demeanor as I introduced myself as the host for the night, while taking in the view.

One girl had wavy blonde hair, generous tits and the curvy belly of an early pregnancy; she greeted me in a French accent, professional and restrained. This was Marie. Her friend Leila had a dark bob, skinny frame, and removed her everyday bra while she was talking to me, to reveal small pert breasts and beautiful pink nipples that I tried not to stare at. Leila was friendly and confident, telling me exactly how to introduce them. She looked me in the eye as she talked about their act...then pressed her fingers deep inside her lacy panties, apparently making some professional adjustment.

"I might need your help after the show," she said in a light American accent as she put on a raunchier bra to match the panties.

"That can be arranged." I spoke calmly but had to plant a hand on the counter to steady myself. In the mirror: silvery hair shaved short at the sides with semierect quiff, that "vintage" T-shirt, dark jeans with a telling bulge for those who cared to look...which part of the package had caught her attention?

I had recently watched a TV comedy in which a male scriptwriter is stuck in a dressing room with the female star of his show, who takes off her bra while chatting with him. That moment flashed through my mind.

Rationally, I knew that in this situation, any act would be getting changed, and a burlesque act would be less shy than some others about doing so in front of the MC. It wasn't a come-on, even though it felt like it. But what was she doing now? Still moving her hand about in her panties for some reason.

I forced myself to look away. The small space was crammed with their stage props: a bouquet of dark red roses; a flowery china tea set spilling from a vintage wicker picnic basket; an abundance of ripe strawberries atop a bag of groceries. These girls did not travel light.

Reno burst into the dressing room. She's a big soft daddy of a woman who you'll find in a sweatshirt in winter, a T-shirt branded with the name of the club in summer, leather harness at any play party within a thousand miles of London...all the genders at once.

"You know we're going to make a mess of the stage?" asked Leila.

"Yes, yes, it's not a problem. Freddy will clear up after the lights go down at the end of your act. And maybe our host will help if we're nice to her. Right?"

"Sure," I said.

"If there's any piss, I'll bring the bucket myself!" Reno said with a laugh, and I wasn't sure if this was likely or not.

They talked about spray-cream and the breakable, antique picnic set, and I wondered what exactly they were going to do. When Reno left, Leila turned to Marie and said, "At the end of the cucumber, can you remember to make allowances for me getting the cork out."

"*Bien sûr.*"

My mind was boggling. When they started to discuss whether Leila should or should not be wearing white panties and she said she'd stopped bleeding and reached down to pull out her menstrual cup, I finally found the tact to leave the room.

I had a pee, did what I could about my hair and picked up free drinks from the grungy barman for the duo. When I returned to the dressing room, Leila and Marie were resplendent in 1950s polka-dot dresses with ribbons in their hair and carefully drawn makeup to extend the line of their eyes. They both wore glossy lipstick and were gleamingly perfect.

"Ready girls?" I asked.

"Sure are!" said Leila. She scooped up the bunch of red roses from the counter and pressed them into my arms, taking the opportunity to brush her hands against mine.

"You shouldn't have," I jested, as her touch buzzed through my body.

"Strew these round the front of the stage for us, sweetie?"

The air between us was electric as I stood waiting for the theme music for my entrance. My mind was not my own. The encounter with Leila, spiced with the pot I'd smoked earlier, was separating me from reality so that the part of me that would usually be planning what to say didn't give a shit.

My theme song belted through the speakers: "Intermission" by the Scissor Sisters. I parted the red velvet curtains and stepped out onto the stage I know so well, my arms full of roses. But I was laughing before anything had happened, before I'd said anything funny. Somehow I redeemed myself, giving a bit of chat, then building up the burlesque act and making the odd joke. It helped that Leila had given me a great line.

"Put away your phones and your cameras," I told the audience, "because there will be no photographs tonight." There was a groan of protest. "Tonight there will be only *mental snapshots*." I loaded the phrase with perversion and they laughed. "Mental snapshots that will stay with you for the rest of your life. If you try to take a photo, the girls will have to kill you.

Which would you prefer? No, don't answer that, you perverts, just put your hands together for...the Paris Paramours!"

As I said this, I cast the flowers down on the stage in an arc. The applause was tremendous. I'd done my job. On came the duo with their wicker basket, as I crossed behind them and quietly slipped out front to watch. No way was I going to miss this act!

They had asked me to give Siggy a CD of four tracks to play for them. The first was a slow, summery number to which they unpacked their picnic before lazing on the ground, feeding each other strawberries. They were both dancers and their graceful movements and charming smiles made it uncertain whether things would get truly raunchy.

By the third track though, the mood shifted. Marie started to doze and Leila gave a devilish smile and threw her arms in the air as a naughty thought occurred to her. She was going to take advantage of her friend's dulled senses to seduce her.

The more I saw, the more difficult it was to act like a professional compere instead of a drooling fan. The dresses they wore must have had special fastenings for their stage act because Leila managed to rip off the top half of Marie's frock and reveal her well-filled bra. The blonde girl kneeled up, as if suddenly awoken by this enforced disrobing, and the two of them exchanged dramatic, smoochy kisses.

Piece by piece, they undressed each other to more traditional striptease music, flinging flowery cotton and delicate lace around the stage with abandon. But Leila—"my" Leila as I was beginning to think of her—needed to keep the upper hand. She bent over the picnic basket and pulled out two long, deep-pink bondage ropes that she wound around her friend's pregnant belly and down around her black lace pants (her one remaining item of clothing), stroking her all the while.

The French girl was now held captive. Leila kissed her delicately, then with a malevolent grin to the audience, grabbed a bunch of roses from the stage, raised them above her head and brought them down with a thrash on the creamy flesh exposed around the ropes. Marie let out little exaggerated cries of pain and astonishment as the flowers came down in rhythm, then she sank to the floor in a faint.

Leila took pity on her. Turning gentle and soothing, she took up a can of cream from their abandoned picnic and sprayed it over Marie's tits, then made a big show of licking it off. I found myself breathing in time with those licks and realized my mouth was wide open. I like a girl who can take control.

But the tables were about to turn. Marie snuck out from under Leila, broke free of her bonds, took up a cucumber from the basket and started to brandish it about. The brunette beauty feigned horror, pointing at the cucumber and shaking her head—apparently it was too big. So Marie took up a gigantic kitchen knife and wielded *that* instead. First Leila widened her eyes in even greater horror and the audience laughed, then her tormentor used the knife to whittle down the cucumber.

Apparently we were building toward the grand finale to which they had alluded in the dressing room.

The French girl first pushed the vegetable into Leila's mouth, watching her suck and lick on it. Then she removed it and moved behind Leila, showing the cucumber to the audience like a magician, before bending to her task. I had a magnificent view of Leila's naked body as she gave in to lust and bent forward to allow her friend full access. She was about to get well and truly fucked and I was soaked with desire. I wanted to do what Marie was doing, as she eased the wet dong between Leila's legs and up, up... One person whooped. I thought maybe it was Siggy. The rest of us were incapable of sound, as Marie pulled the cucumber in and out of Leila's tight pussy, somehow retaining her poise all the while. We were each glued to the spot, watching in awed and delighted silence as this full-on sex show thrust toward its climax.

That cucumber was having quite an impact on Leila's entire body. As she struggled to stay standing, her carefully composed features now betrayed a hint of her genuine enjoyment of the fucking she was getting. The thrusting grew faster and faster, the music built to a crescendo and, right on cue, the two girls shuddered together in ecstasy. At that moment, Leila somehow managed to pop open a bottle of sparkling wine and spray it dramatically into the audience.

Released from the spell and showered with its magic simultaneously, the audience cried out or laughed in delight. The butches and trans guys standing in the front shouted, "Oi!" as they shook wine from their carefully waxed hair, but really, who could object after what we had just witnessed?

I sprinted up the steps to the wings, ready to go on as soon as the girls came off. But when they appeared, stark naked, from the wrong direction, I realized they must have exited into the audience before following me up the steps and through the dressing room.

"Well done!" I whooped. "That was amazing." Marie nodded coolly; Leila smirked and winked. I picked my way through the devastation on the stage, trying not to stomp on the irreplaceable china.

"Did you enjoy that?" I asked into the microphone. The crowd roared. I was giddy myself so I knew how they felt. "Give them another round of applause!"

As the clapping burst forth, Marie and Leila pulled open the drapes to take another curtain call. I stood there, watching them in all their glory, curtseying inches away from me. As they left the stage once more, I said to the audience, "Well, I think I need to have a lie-down now...probably backstage." I winked as I bowed and took my leave.

The two performers seemed calm and neat now in their lingerie, putting things away in boxes and bags. Had my moment passed?

"I'll go and clear up," I said.

"Come back when you're done," said Leila, giving me an intense look that could mean only one thing. Marie raised an eyebrow at her. I just nodded.

I tried to ignore the fact that my hands were shaking as I helped a mohawked young Freddy to clear the stage. She'd brought the cleaning gear from behind the bar and was already energetically engaged in her task. I wrapped the honored cucumber in paper towels before dropping it into the bin with the kind of respect I might give a dead bird in the garden.

"I just went and had a wank," said Freddy, with her usual lack of inhibition. "I couldn't wait."

She must have been quick about it.

"I think I may have something better lined up," I told her. "I think..." I could barely say the words. "I think Leila is interested in me."

"Oh, boy. Oh, girl! They are both so hot. Good luck!"

I nipped into the unisex loos to wash my hands. I hadn't been in a relationship for a while and I took every chance I could for sex, but this was an opportunity sent from heaven, so good that I didn't quite believe it...until I passed Marie on her own at the bar and realized she had vacated the dressing room to give Leila some space.

After hosting the cabaret on and off for the past year, I've had a few fantasies about what could happen in that room, but this would be the first time I'd put it to the test. I knocked and entered. Leila was standing there, still in her panties, but she had removed the little lacy bra. She leaned back against the counter. "You came back," she said, smiling. "My silver fox."

I didn't trust myself to speak. I tried to make an asset of silence, cupping her face in my hand. Her skin was warm and smooth; her deep, dark eyes cheeky and seductive. I loved that she had just revealed everything to everyone but saved the after-party for me.

"You had better be packing," she told me.

I licked her face. Don't ask me why. I just wanted to do it and I had the feeling I could do anything I wanted. I pressed into her so she could feel my hard cock through my jeans, its head pushing against her crotch through the thin lace of her panties. She gasped. I touched my lips to hers and they opened, our tongues meeting hungrily. I knew her performance had made us both hot in different ways.

"Did you come onstage?" I asked.

Leila shook her head. "It's a *performance*," she said.

"You got fucked with that cucumber in front of all those horny people by that gorgeous friend of yours and you didn't come?"

"I need a butch to make me come," she said, with an odd, ironic smile that meant it might be true or might just be a tease. I didn't mind either way. It was a game I was willing to play.

Her lipstick was still shining and I honed back in on that luscious mouth, her wet lips opening to mine. She was ready to melt for me. I slipped a hand into those gossamer panties and gasped at how wet she was. Her hips pushed forward and my fingers slid into that delicious cunt. "*Ohhh*," she moaned from the back of her throat as we continued to kiss like hungry picnickers.

Then she pulled her mouth from mine to murmur, "I don't

have much time. Marie gets tired…with the pregnancy." She grabbed at my hair and spoke right in my face. "Just fuck me with your cock. Fuck me hard."

I didn't need to be asked again. I turned her around to fold her lithe body over the counter, unzipped and groaned as I inched aside those lacy panties to press my silicone dick into her wet cunt, watching it slide in just like that cucumber, watching Leila's face contort in the mirror, so different from her controlled, onstage expressions.

As I pressed into her, she pushed harder against me, taking my whole cock inside her in a hungry, sliding ride that rocked us both, till we were buckling against the counter. With one hand, I held the base of the dildo pressed against my own clit and levered the shaft against the front wall of her pussy, thinking of that fat cucumber, that keen crowd. I wrapped the other arm under her, teased at a nipple, and was rewarded with more thrusts back and forth from those dancer's hips of hers.

It was all my fantasies come true, this near-naked girl taking all she could get from me, but I knew we had just one chance to get it right because she would soon be gone, back to her exotic world of Paris cabaret.

We were locked together for sweaty, staggering minutes, Leila's gasps and moans building, my cock moving inside her, my swollen cunt fit to burst, my right hand moving on her clit. Then she screamed and buckled—and so did I.

"Ohhh, you're good," I murmured in her ear as I collapsed on top of her.

"I told you I needed it," she whispered in reply.

A sudden flash of light bounced off the mirror like an echo from the heavens. For a moment I thought I was hallucinating. Then I saw that Marie was taking photos and Reno was positioned behind her, shaking her head in mock disapproval.

Crowded behind them, to my chagrin, were Tatiana and both her lovers, plus Freddy, Siggy...and the grungy guy from behind the bar. How long had they been there?

"*Only mental snapshots*," I barked at Marie, in an effort to maintain my dignity, but my voice sounded oddly staccato in the aftermath of orgasm, my cock still twitching idly inside Leila.

The Frenchwoman arched a plucked eyebrow. "Taxi's here," she announced, as she turned on her heel, parting our little audience, cool as a cucumber.

ANONYMOUS

BD Swain

Sometimes you just want to be fucked by someone you don't know and will never see again.

You shower after it's already dark. You get dressed. You go out, jamming your fists into your jacket pockets. You walk fast, digging your heels into the sidewalk, and you keep your head down. You know where you're going.

There's a club. You have to know where it is. You walk down that alley and then it's the second door on the left, down in the basement.

Cabs are pulling up and letting people out and letting other people stumble in. You can smell the river over here and it doesn't smell good.

Take out the pack of cigarettes and hit it on your palm but put it back in your pocket unopened. Just go in.

Down the steps and straight to the bar; you order a scotch, neat, and drink it fast. You have that look on your face: furtive, eyes dashing around. She isn't here. She would never be here. And that's why you are here now.

Who will it be? Find someone who looks like she can take you, and stare, head tilted down. Look up at her with your brow furrowed and that open, pleading look in your eyes. The first one will look away. It's okay. Let her look away, find another one.

The right one will stare back. The right one will know what this means. The right one will stare at you and then go to the bar and order a drink. And you'll order another drink, but sip it this time. Squeeze the glass hard in your hand like you're trying to break it and sip it slow. Let the booze sit on your tongue and burn a little before you swallow it down. Let her watch you.

When you finish your drink, look for her again. Leave a tip on the bar and turn around. Push your way through the crowd. You will feel her grab your elbow before you make it to the door. Let her stop you.

She pulls you back toward the bar but keeps going. Off to the left there are more stairs leading to a deeper basement. Stone butches are playing pool and don't you dare bump up against one or you'll get the shit kicked out of you and not in the way you want.

She's getting her coat. You turn around and she slams you up against the cinder-block wall and grinds her knee between your legs. She pushes into you, squeezing you between her and the wall and it's hard to breathe. She is sucking your mouth. Not kissing you but sucking your tongue; everything is spinning.

"Let's go," she says, and you follow her.

Outside she walks right by the cabs. The street is dark. There are people fucking in doorways, but she keeps walking. There's a chain-link fence at the edge of the river. As you're tossed against it, the sound of it shocks you, the metal rippling like a wave down the empty streets in loud crashes.

She yanks up your shirt; her mouth is on your breasts for only a few seconds before she turns you around and shoves you against the cold metal. She pulls at your belt and jerks your pants down to your knees. As she fumbles with you, the links in the fence pinch on your belly and your breasts. You bring your hands up and wrap your fingers tightly, clinging to the fence and letting her tug on you.

She bites your neck; you can feel her bruising you. She wets her fingers on your cunt. One hand, then both hands move between your legs. A wet finger backs up to your ass and she slides it in, pressing against you with her hips and rocking her hand and body into you. Her other hand, her whole hand, is on your cunt. She is rubbing you off. You want her to fill you, but you have no say right now.

You hear the sound of a car and then you're in the headlights for a second as a cab swings a U-turn and heads off. She's laughing. "They won't even know what they were looking at: people fucking, yes, but girls or boys? They'll assume boys. Girls don't fuck on the street like this, right?"

The thought of having been caught in the lights makes you crazy. You want to get off. You want her to get you off, but you don't want this to end.

She bends her knees and wraps herself around you. Still fucking you in the ass, she finally pushes her other hand into your cunt and you feel yourself open up for her immediately. More fingers move into you and still you want more. You want her inside you up to her wrist. You want her whole fucking hand inside you.

You are hanging on the fence now, your body letting go and the muscles in your arms straining and holding you up. The cold metal fence bites into your fingers and your arms start to shake. "You're yelling," she says with amusement. You got lost. You got completely lost tonight. Just what you needed.

There is no exchange of numbers or names. "I don't want to be fucked," she says, "but that was fun." And then she walks away.

WOMAN-TIME

Rebecca Lynne Fullan

She walked into the classroom late as usual, a tight black skirt riding halfway up her ass. She almost always wore heels, and today was no exception. Red heels so sharp and pointy you could've used them as pencils, if they'd been leaded. I watched her black skirt and her red heels and her brown legs and then refocused on my notebook, hunching my shoulders under their light-jacket shield. In my case, bare skin was a risk rarely worth taking.

She was smart, too, picking up quickly where we were in the discussion and piercing the conversation with words and phrases too well chosen to annoy with their directness. This did annoy me, of course, and her toes annoyed me as she pushed one shoe off with the other foot, and her ankle annoyed me as she rubbed the arch of her now-free foot against it. I looked at her hair, a contained firework of an Afro, and I glanced at her shoulders under the red tank top that completed her outfit. I avoided looking at her face. I knew it would be beautiful. And smug.

Instead, too distracted now to follow the discussion, I scribbled a sketch into my notebook; just a few quick, angry lines: pointy cat-face, long back, tail. Slash-slash-slash for stripes. Tiger. Then squat, rounded, all low-to-ground, long lined snout. Badger.

The section ended and I gathered my things in hasty disorganization, out the door before I'd even put my backpack on properly.

She caught up with me on the campus green. She'd taken off her heels and was holding them in one hand by the straps. Her feet looked good against the grass, like they belonged there.

"Hey," she said. "You late for something?"

"No—"

"Just in a hurry," she finished on my behalf. I could hear the smile in her voice, glanced quickly up to catch its edge. Her face was beautiful. And smug. Sure of herself, of what she thought she knew.

"I have a lot to do."

"I could see a little of what you were drawing. Do you have more like that?"

I didn't answer. I walked a little faster. My notebook worked its way free of my arms and she caught it before it hit the ground. I stopped, unwilling to ask for it back, and instead began stuffing the things I'd been carrying into my backpack. Then I stood waiting for my notebook but not reaching for it.

She looked at me and opened the cover. Beside and across and over my notes were the pictures. Animals and more animals. Small, big, predators, prey. Women's bodies working in and out, hinted at and started. Most broken in some way: arms twisting and elongated, heads vanished, legs bent at odd angles. A few were explicitly changing, feet growing claws, fur sprouting. She closed the cover and handed it back to me.

"You're really good," she said. "But how do you get such

good grades in Anthro, if this is what you're doing during class?"

"I don't get good grades," I said.

"Yeah, you do," she insisted mildly. "I saw your test paper when it came back last week."

I put the notebook into my backpack, zipped it up and started walking again. She stood where she was.

"Hey," she called after me, "I moved into Forest House this semester. I bet we'd give you some commissions if you wanted. They've been talking about having murals and paintings and stuff, and this would be perfect."

Forest House was this co-op of mostly lesbian wiccan types. Bitches. Girls playing with dolls, that's what they were, and calling it real life. Just the thought of those bitches and their crystals and their spirit animal totem shit made my gorge rise. I swallowed it again.

"We're having a party this weekend. If you wanted to come by."

I turned back to look at her. She was still standing there, beautiful, smug, and hopeful. Her shoes dangled crimson from her fingers. She was not small. She took up space and she smiled.

"Fuck Forest House," I said, loud enough for her to hear. I turned again and made my clumsy, fast way back to my dorm room.

My dorm was not a co-op. It was concrete and tall, bland to the eye and the touch, but insulating, which is what I required of it. I ran up the stairs to my room and threw my backpack to the floor. The room was small and crammed, but I liked it. It was decorated, multicolored scarves strewn and hung everywhere. I had gotten some of those washable wall crayons and scrawled lines and colors all over the wall, but no discernable shapes like in my notebook. No good to have specific suggestions staring at me all the time. I felt good about the space, though no one but me ever came in.

I dropped to the floor, onto a braided rug one of my aunts had made, round and spiraling and a little rough. I pulled off my jacket, shirt and bra, and lay with my stomach and breasts pressed to the rug. The prickly soft grains scratched at my nipples. I pulled open my jeans and shoved my hand inside. My vulva and clit were warm and swollen. I touched them through my underwear and quick pleasure stabbed me. I rubbed until my breath came fast, pushing my breasts harder against the rug. I rolled over onto my back and arched against the rug. My first two fingers stroked firm and slow, all the way down and up again, and then focused, circling and circling my clit through the fabric.

My breath stopped. I pushed against my hand, sucked in more breath and came, in fast, shuddering waves.

"Fuck, fuck, fuck," I muttered. I got up, wiped my forehead with one hand, left my jeans on the floor with my shirt and bra. It hadn't been enough: not the kind of arousal that would be satisfied with orgasms, not the kind of anger that I could stave with odd outbursts on the green. My body was quivering, under the skin, way under. The basic level, the level almost nobody can feel. Muscles, bones quivering.

Inside your body, there is a whole code, everything working together, keeping you *you*. Every cell cooperates, participates, lives and dies according to this, so that you stay perceptibly yourself. Everyone knows this, right?

My code is fucked. My code is magic. I don't stay myself. There is no center.

My body shook, convulsed. I lay on the bed. The pain started, like a crazy burn-itch all through me, like a muscle you want to stretch, like a cramp you can't relieve, pain growing and unremitting. I was consumed and I panted in it.

Then compression. Small, small, small. Quivering, twitching. Settling. Now relief. No more pain. No more words. Hunger. Heartbeat. Fast. Run run run. Skitter. Forever. Food. Small opening. Squeeze. Run run run. Fast. Fear, frozen. Big eyes big heat near me. Frozen, frozen, fear. Claws at me, flying. Run run run. Fast fast. Run.

I came back to myself in the basement of my dorm, naked and covered in sweat and small scratches. I moved quickly, too quickly still, and found the simple pullover dress I'd hidden behind the washing machine. I tried to keep my clothes widely scattered and available, but of course it was hit or miss. I smelled my skin and thought back as best I could. I hunted around and found a small pile of droppings with a finger. I hated mouse-times. Mouse-times were dangerous and scary, especially because some assholes insisted on sneaking kittens into their dorm rooms. But really, all times were dangerous and scary, to me, to others. Even woman-times. Maybe woman-times the most, because in woman-times I knew.

I made my way back up to my hall on shaky legs. I slipped into the bathroom and showered, then pulled my dress back over my wet body and headed back to my own room. I fell into bed, piled on covers despite the stuffy heat and slept.

The next day I found a flyer for the Forest House party, jammed in with hundreds of other flyers on a corkboard. It was light pink, with a drawing of a woman who seemed to be turning into a tree, her curves winding and sensual, melding with bark and trunk and pushing into the ground. FUN FUN FUN, the flyer said in big letters to the side of the tree woman. FOREST HOUSE FALL MIXER, SATURDAY SEPTEMBER 18TH, 10-??? The poster made me smile, then laugh. I touched the tree woman with a finger and traced her outer lines. What would it be like to be a tree-person, a plant-person? Safer, or would you have to rush to soil and take root and hope to be large enough not to be stepped on or eaten? Perhaps it was all more or less the same. Still, irrationally, I liked her; felt she had a freedom, a pleasure, something I did not. I took the poster down and hid it in my room.

For minutes together, later that week, looking at the tree woman's form in half darkness, touching my own body and rising and falling, sea-like, I felt something like forgiveness for those crystal-wielding, herb-taking, cunt-licking bitches who prayed, secretly and openly, for the changing of their limbs and the release of animal-selves, animal-muscles.

But even as I opened, ascended, came and came again, I shut off the sensation of forgiveness when it approached myself.

I went to the party. Wore jeans and a Harry Potter T-shirt, with an open black hoodie over it. The shirt was kind of a joke. Women and a few fey-looking men hung around in doorways drinking spiced ales and fruit wines and touching lightly. There were candles, incense, a couple circles of people earnestly casting spells. I saw a woman on all fours by a couch, stretching her back out and making a little growling noise. I took a few steps toward her. She was white, really pale, with reddish-brown hair. A little like Polly, but skinnier. She looked at me, human eyes all dilated, and snarled. I took a step back again.

"She's totally into her wolf totem." I turned around and saw one of the boys, his face a mass of acne but friendly underneath. "It's kinda freaky at first, huh? But like, don't worry, if she gets really feral, we can touch her with silver and she comes back." He held out his arm and showed me the thin silver bracelet on his wrist. I put out my hand and touched it, running my finger over the surface. I raised my eyes to his, pulled back the veil a little and smiled.

He left the conversation pretty damn quick after that. The

wolf girl had gotten tired and was curled up at the end of the couch on the floor, wiggling her butt a little like she had a tail. I turned away and wandered through the house, down the hall to the stairwell.

"Hi," she said, and I was startled. She came down from the first landing on the stairs, mostly in shadow. I watched her outline: hair, shoulders, hips. She came out into the light on the first floor. She was wearing a navy-blue dress, simple but as tight and sexy as most everything else she wore. She wore it carelessly, wore the swell of her ass and her breasts like they were easy to carry, nothing to bother about. But she was still wearing heels, these a sort of faux-snakeskin in shades of tan. Her feet seemed to shade up from them, the lighter bottom visible against the tan, rising to the richer brown of her top-skin. Her feet were so much safer to look at, but not that safe. Also, it was weird to keep staring at someone's feet.

"I'm glad you came," she said. I looked at her face, her eyes. Her eyes were not smug. They were open, welcoming, dark.

"I saw somebody being a wolf," I said, I don't know why. Her smile blossomed out like sun coming through a cloud.

"Yeah, some people are a little showy about the magic stuff. You want a drink, or something?"

"Okay," I said. She moved easily through the more crowded part of the house then disappeared into the kitchen. I watched her strong, wide back and the sway of her ass. She came back with two beers. I sipped and swallowed the sharpness.

"Look," she said, "I know you're a senior, right? So you were here before I was, and I figure maybe you used to hang out at Forest House, and—"

"Not really," I said.

"But you maybe knew Polly." She was less confident now, staring down into her beer can. "I heard she was kinda—she could be a nasty bitch, especially to women she was messing around with. So I thought maybe that's why you don't like Forest House. I'm glad you came, and I'm sorry if something fucked up happened to you here."

My skin started to buzz. Jesus, twice in one week? That was rare. I set my beer down, carefully, against the wall. It was less likely somebody would kick it over that way.

"I gotta go," I said.

"Oh, shit, I'm sorry."

"No, it's not—I've just gotta go." I began moving through the crowd. Right now I felt buzzing, tingling, a sort of pre-painful ache in muscles and joints. Soon it would be more, but I could tell I had time to get out. A stabbing cramp hit as I reached the door and I stopped with my hand on the doorpost, bent, waiting.

"Hey, you okay?" It was the silver-bracelet guy from before. "You should have some water, sit down awhile."

"Not drunk," I gasped. I pushed away his solicitous hand and made it out the door. The night was cool, but I was sweating. The ache grew stronger in my feet, knees, ass, back. I ran, a strange, loping gait, aided by urgency but hindered by pain and the stretch in my bones. There was an almost-forest at the edge of campus—deep enough to hide for a while, not deep enough for much hunting, if it was a hunter coming. I could get there.

I panted as I ran, sweat dripping down my neck and my back. I could feel my skin soaking in it, letting it out and marinating itself. I peeled off my hoodie and let it fall. I reached down and pulled off my shoes; my feet were all pins and needles and wanted to be free. My vision was changing, sliding, shifting. For a moment I thought I knew a wolf-time was coming and I laughed to be so suggestible. Then my tongue went heavy in my mouth and my thoughts slanted and I bent over, close to all fours but not quite touching the ground in front. I was moving faster now, faster than I could in woman-times. I was at the trees and then the pain was blinding for a minute and then I was sleek, sleek, fast, energy straight through, shooting silver out to ground and *pleasure*—

Pleasure of movement, pleasure of speed, pleasure of sweat on fur, heavy pleasure, feet quick and smell all over. Nothing to worry, all moving and smelling and listening and pausing. Yes hunger mouth hunger stomach hunger pit hunger. Turning turning smelling stillness eager. Other-kill yes growl gobble spin chase. Smell of not-prey, smell, too-strong, melt vanish go. Marking, smelling, moving. Not-prey still. Smelling. Knowing.

I know. I am still. Looking. Stillness. Looking at her, in her stillness. Alive, right here, surface. Fear and pleasure. Deep. Strong. She opens her fingers, at her side. I want to smell them. Step. Step. Close now. Nose raised. Nose to fingers. Strong smell, deep smell. Sweat and the brass tang of her just-starting menses. I can see her with new sharpness. Must be coyote-time. Woman-time things bleed through in coyote-time. I keep my stillness and her eyes. Then I run.

When I came to myself again I was crouched at the far edge of the forest. I sat, exhausted, in my own sweat, feeling moss and dry leaves against my knees and thighs. I stayed there for a moment, letting my breathing come down, muscles quivering under skin. Then I remembered. Had she really been there? Had I imagined? I turned around, slowly, getting to my feet. I could barely see in the early dawn. I couldn't smell a thing, the worst part of woman-time. Humans can't smell for shit.

I figured my clothes were back closer to the campus, maybe shredded a bit but hopefully wearable. I started walking back, slowly, touching the trees as I passed. After a long change, a full night like that one, I was always both tired and strangely rested.

The sun coming up was warm and bright. I watched it coloring in all the night grays of the almost-forest.

Back at my clothes, there she was, dozing against a tree with the remnants of my Harry Potter shirt under her arm. I tried to wear mostly clothes I didn't care about, but sometimes I felt perverse. I watched her, the pull of her party dress over her boobs and her belly, the fabric carelessly riding up her thighs. I looked at my shirt in the crook of her elbow. She opened her eyes. We watched each other.

She held my shirt out and I took it, examining the strain, the rip caused by a claw as I worked my way free. I pulled it over my head. I started to walk away.

"Your pants are over there," she said, pointing. I saw them and moved toward them. "Wait," she said. "Don't get them yet."

I stared at her. "You're not scared," I accused. "You oughta be."

"I'm scared," she said.

"You're into this, it turns you on."

"Yeah," she said.

"It's fucking scary shit," I said. "It's not a game. I turn into animals, all kinds of animals; did you think I was a werewolf like that stupid girl? She's not anything; she's just a human being who likes being trippy and weird."

"You were a coyote."

"Yes."

"But you're not always a coyote."

"Do I look like a coyote right now?"

"No." She smiled.

I sighed. I lowered myself to a crouch. I was tired. "I'm lots of different kinds of animals," I said. "Some of them, I don't even think are real. Some are definitely extinct. I don't always know, when I change, what I am, what the English name is or the human idea about it. I can't make it stop, usually, and I don't decide when it happens, and there's no rule, that I can tell, except that—it happens when I'm feeling something. Not one thing in particular, just—strong things. And not even always then. I don't know why." She nodded. I sucked in a breath, dug my fingernails into my palms, and said it fast. "I turned into a bear when Polly broke up with me. And I scratched her. Badly. That's really why she transferred."

She laughed. I blinked at her. Then I laughed. I landed full on the ground, with a bump, and laughed.

"It was bad," I insisted when I'd stopped laughing. "I mean, yeah, she was a bitch, she really was, but I attacked her. As a bear. It's not…"

"You didn't kill her," she pointed out. "I mean, you might have, but you didn't."

"Bully for me," I said.

"I mean it."

"You don't seem scared."

"I am," she said. She reached and put her hand on my thigh. She crawled her fingers up and brushed them over my pubic hair, this way and that, her eyes rising to mine. "I'm scared," she said. She cupped her fingers over my vulva, and I could feel it warm and swell beneath them. "Is this okay?" She waited a moment. "It turns me on because it's magic and because it's yours."

I was quiet. I felt the throb and pulse push out from my center to her hand. She took her hand away.

"I want to fuck you," I said, looking at the grass under my fingertips and not at her. "When I see you in class, the smart things you say, you get under the skin of things. And your hair and your feet in those high heels and the clothes you wear. The curves of your ass and your boobs and your belly. And the shape of your jaw and the strength of your back. I shouldn't fuck anybody, this thing that I am. But I want to fuck you."

I could hear her breathing as I spoke and then she was on me like a wild thing, leaping and pressing and tumbling me back against the floor of the almost-forest. Her hand returned to my labia and my clit, drawing me up against her like a magnet. My back arched and my hips pushed forward. She bit me and scratched me with her other hand and I giggled helplessly and then grew still.

I felt stillness, circling, and a throbbing hunger, great, fierce, in the center of my body, sucking away my breath and giving it back in bursts. The noises in my throat were strange but human, for all their ferocity. I felt her middle finger dipping and playing at the opening of my cunt, teasing the puckered edge and sending a jolt straight from there to her palm against my clit. My hips surged and bobbed like a toy boat in a rough current, and I came in sudden, pulsing jolts, and then I forced myself back, down, away.

"Take off your dress," I said hoarsely, and she looked at me and did. Her bra was purple and satiny, and her underwear was a plain cotton bikini. She undid her bra and pulled her underwear off. I was on her breasts as soon as I could see them, raisin-dark nipple sucked hard between my lips. She made a quick, deep, grunting sound, and then a higher, floating cry. She got back her breath. "Your period's about to start," I told her. "I could smell it."

She laughed softly, breathlessly, but I saw a real stab of fear in her eyes for the first time. She didn't hide it, just looked at me as she pressed her back against a tree trunk and parted her thighs.

"I like it deep and slow," she said.

I circled her breasts with my mouth and her cunt with my hand, taking in the shape and the soft folds that surrounded me.

Different from mine, larger, more contoured. I swept my fingers over the top of her clit, felt her shudder and pressed in harder, circling and finding the opening, slick and warm. I straddled her thigh and rubbed my own cunt against her, drawing out bursts of color under my skin, all up and down. My thoughts whirled and splintered, and I let my first two fingers slide inside her, deep and slow. Her arm came around my back and gripped me, hard. We rode each other and I pressed her, deeply, inside and out, the heel of my hand and my thumb searching out her clit. I lost my balance against her leg, dropping to the side of her. I closed my eyes then opened them again to watch her face. Her mouth was opening, wider and wider, and she was almost silent, straining against my hand. She laughed, suddenly, and then choked on the end of it, and I felt her clench and rise and come, the tension in her bursting like a bubble, opening like the new leaf on a tree, fresh, green, fiercely connected.

I pulled my fingers out of her, showed her the blood at the very tips, and then put them between my lips to suck them clean. Threatening, warning, daring, accepting—I couldn't have said. Woman-time without words. Her eyes were locked on mine, and when I ate her blood they lit like I had touched her. She groaned and pushed me back, grabbing my ass in both her hands and squeezing, lifting my hips toward her and pressing her face into my crotch, nuzzling and licking and then rising to kiss my mouth. She lingered there, long and sweet and dizzying, and her hand slid between my legs and stroked me until I came again and again, easily, without strain, fire-bursts in a show I did not have to control.

We lay on the ground afterward, separate and quiet, our fingers touching. At last I stood up and began looking for my pants. We got dressed, still silent. She picked a few leaves out of her hair, steadied herself against a tree trunk, and looked at me again. Her eyes asked questions. I wanted to answer them. I felt a change at a distance, hovering, not yet here, something with wings.

"Will you come back with me?" I asked. "I want to show you my room."

She took my hand and squeezed 'til I could feel the bones beneath.

"Yes," she answered. "Yes."

KITTY AND THE CAT

Amelia Thornton

It was near midnight when I got there, and I knew she could see me when I walked in. And by "walked in," I mean *sashayed* in, hips swinging, head high, every curve perfectly contained and displayed and inviting the gaze of every person in that room. I knew she could see me, and I knew she would want it. She just didn't know what it was yet.

Lynn had told me about her, said she'd just moved into the flat below, seemed ever so sweet and unassuming and just generally *nice*. I like nice girls. Especially when I can make them be so not-nice when I try. Of course it only seemed neighborly that Lynn would invite her to the party, and of course she had warned me to "be good," but good is not something I am particularly capable of, especially when I am presented with a specimen so utterly, unquestionably adorable. Out of the corner of my eye I could see her, staring, trying hard to compose herself and continue her small talk, but not quite able to. She couldn't help it. Girls like her never can.

Of course she would submit; there was no question about that. She would be on her knees, her tongue caressing the slick shine of my heels, her worshipful eyes looking up at me, begging me to fuck her ass and cane her thighs and do whatever I wanted with her, whatever that was. She would tell me how much she needed it, tell me she was mine, tell me her whole body and being belonged to me entirely. But that's never the best bit. The best bit is always the part when they just don't know they're submissive yet, when they haven't realized the true equality of inequality and the beautiful release of giving themselves over. This chase, this game, this revealing of what I always know and they never do, this is the part that makes the blood pump through my veins. And I intended to savor every tiny, minuscule moment of it.

Across the room, I could see Lynn scowling at me, annoyed I had ignored her primly conservative costume advice and turned up in my own creation. I just smiled good-naturedly and gave her a little wave, mentally altering her entire pirate wench outfit to be at least six inches shorter and possibly two sizes tighter. Bless her. She didn't *really* think I was going to miss an opportunity like this, did she?

The sheer beauty of costume parties is that they make it utterly acceptable, if not mandatory, to dress like a complete slut, and though sluttery is usually what I pride my girls on, not myself, I felt it rude not to get in the spirit of things. After much deliberation, I had decided on Catwoman, since I already owned the outfit, and I knew it was just what I needed to make Cute Little Neighbor aware of what I intended for her. As a nod to the flimsy excuse for head-to-toe perversion my character allowed, I even had a matching black cat-eye mask, but the beauty of the outfit was in the suit. Every curve of my body was coated in a thick sheen of polished black latex, clinging to

KITTY AND THE CAT

me like a second skin, each limb a smooth length of blackness; my feet were encased in tightly laced six-inch-high boots. My ivory-white breasts were crushed into an unbearable cleavage, revealed by the temptingly lowered zipper bisecting my entire torso, undone just enough to display what I wanted, but also to hint at what was beneath. She would certainly want what was beneath, I knew that much.

I was pondering how long to leave it before going to fetch her, and how forward to be when I did, when I heard a small, timid voice at my side.

"Hello."

I turned, blinking in surprise to see her standing there already. *So the prey thinks she can be the predator, hmm?* Her eyes were round and expressive, a deep brown framed by long lashes, and there was a sprinkling of freckles across her rounded nose. Her neat brown bob was topped with a pair of cat ears looking suspiciously like bachelorette party accessories, and the rest of the outfit was a plain black leotard, shiny black tights and a homemade cat tail made from a wire hanger wrapped in furry fabric. Around her neck was a pastel-pink kitty collar, trimmed with diamanté, with a little metal tag in the shape of a heart. I do like an attention to detail. The paws were what got me though: safety-pinned with ribbon to each of her leotard sleeves hung two furry black mitts, stitched with pretty, pink satin paw prints, looking alluringly as if they would render the hands quite useless if put on properly. Oh, my poor, helpless, pretty little kitty...

"Hello," I replied, half smiling in amusement at how perfectly innocent she looked like that, half at how depraved I knew she would become. "What's your name?"

She looked a little awkward, as if taken off balance by my simplest of questions, or perhaps more by the tone of an adult

48

talking to a small but adorable child, instead of one adult talking to another.

"Susie."

"Well, Susie, it's very nice to meet you. You've just moved in downstairs, haven't you?"

"Yeah, a couple of weeks ago. It seems lovely here; everyone's really friendly and everything, not like where I used to live; my neighbors were just a nightmare, and Lynn's ever so sweet to invite me to her party, and..."

"Yes, she is," I cut in smoothly, almost able to taste the nervousness of her babbling. "I would quite like you to go and get me a drink, Susie. Vodka and soda, with fresh lime. Half-full with ice. Will you go and do that for me?"

Her eyes widened as if she was not quite sure if I really had just interrupted her and told her what to do. Well, asked her, really. Telling would come later.

"Oh...um, of course. Certainly. I'll be right back."

"Good girl," I said with a smile, watching her cheeks flush as she scurried away, her little coat-hanger tail swaying from side to side. Oh, she was just too, too perfect. I had tried in the past to take the small-talk route, exchange pleasantries, discuss preferences. It usually worked out all right in the end, but it was just so terribly, tediously dull. It was much more fun to start off by knocking them sideways and see what happened, and besides, I'd never been wrong yet. I always know when a nice girl wants to be bad for me.

A few moments later, she returned, my drink in one hand and hers in the other, an expectant smile on her face.

"Thank you," I said as I took it, making sure to look straight into her big brown eyes in a way I knew would make her squirm. She looked so beautiful like that. "I do like your costume, Susie. Did you make it yourself?"

"Yes." She looked a little embarrassed at having made her own costume, not realizing that was the very thing that made me want her even more, that innocence that just couldn't be bought.

"It's very nice. Why haven't you got your paws on though?" I inquired, knowing full well why not.

"Well, they're just a bit tricky to do things with you see. Everyone was getting a bit fed up with me getting black fluff in the Doritos, so I just took them off!" She grinned shyly, tugging at the fuzzy paws. "They were more for effect than for wearing, really."

"Well, a real kitten wouldn't have the choice to take her paws off, would she?" I remarked, admiring the way this made her shift her weight from one foot to the other. "She wouldn't be drinking from a glass, but from a little saucer on the floor, and curling up at her mistress's feet like a good little kitty, having her ears stroked and her neck tickled. That is, if you were good. I think perhaps you should put them on, don't you?"

She stared at me, as if trying to decide if I was being serious or not. I could see all of the thoughts running through her head, wondering if I meant what she thought she'd heard. I just waited.

"Well..." she began slowly, "will you hold my drink for me?"

Oh, that first victory always tasted the sweetest.

"Of course." I took the glass from her, watching her awkwardly slip her hands inside the pink satin lining of the paws. She had certainly done a good job, to bother lining them at all. It made me wonder how much she enjoyed the thought of putting her hands inside there, feeling herself just that little bit immobilized, not being able to grip and hold and reach.

"Can I have my drink back now, please?"

It almost made me want to laugh, her trusting naïveté.

"I thought we established kitties don't drink from glasses, but from saucers?"

"Did we?"

"Yes."

She looked at me, a sudden panic flashing across her features as she realized what I meant, at the same time wondering if that really *was* what I meant. "Don't worry though," I soothed her, "I'll fetch a saucer for you, seeing as you can't do it yourself. Wait there…and don't move."

I made sure the last words held just the right amount of force to let her know that I expected her to do as I said, and left her there frantically imagining all of the horrors a saucer could bring. I kept glancing back at her while I went to the kitchen, and sure enough, she didn't move an inch. Such a good girl. I surveyed the contents of her glass, which didn't look like anything I wanted my kitten to drink, so discarded it. I felt a real kitty should probably drink milk, but seeing as mine was a special one, she deserved something a little more special. A rummage round the back of Lynn's fridge yielded some rather interesting-looking white chocolate liqueur—most likely just as bad as the junk I had poured away, but at least of a somewhat higher quality. Delicately balancing my saucer, I returned to my pet, who was obediently standing just where I had left her.

"Have you been a good kitty while I've been gone?" I inquired, smiling at how the very words made her fidget.

"Um, I…er…"

She didn't know what to say. Slowly, languidly I sat myself down on one of the dining chairs that had been dragged into the lounge to provide more seating, observing that, oddly enough, the entire area around us seemed to have gathered quite a crowd. I imagined Lynn was fuming at the "spectacle" I was

making, but I didn't care. There was something deliciously satisfying about humiliating a girl in public, especially in front of a
crowd of strangers. I knew Lynn's friends were pretty easygoing,
so nobody was going to have a problem, but it made it more
excruciating for little Susie to have all these people looking at
her while she did all the things she didn't realize she was going
to do yet.

I placed the saucer on the floor.

"Drink it."

I looked up at her, standing there above me, with an expression of such sheer mortification on her face I wanted to kiss her
right then and there.

"Um, it's on the floor?" she responded uneasily.

"I know. And you will be too in a minute when you get down
there and drink it. Don't you want to be a good little kitten for
me?"

This would be the turning point, the tip over the edge. No
sane woman would get on her hands and knees and lick from a
saucer in a crowded room unless she really, really needed this.

"Yes."

Her voice was a hoarse whisper, almost inaudible, but a
sound that sent sparks down my spine. Beneath my glistening
latex I could feel a slick sheen of sweat on my skin, the rubber
seeming to cling even tighter as I absorbed that beautiful moment
of admittance. She would be mine.

"I think you should perhaps get on the floor and drink the
milk I've brought you then, don't you?"

It was almost as if I could see the devil and angel battling on
her shoulders. To give in was to shame herself, to show all these
people she had just met that she wanted to be told what to do
by a woman in shiny rubber and six-inch heels, but to give in
was also to give up, to surrender her self-control and let herself

be carried away with the calming pleasure of complete obedience. I don't even know which one was the devil, and which the angel, but one of them won, and she gradually, painfully lowered herself to her knees, her cheeks burning. I glanced at our fellow guests, most of whom didn't seem that interested anymore, since the subtleties of mind games were beyond their comprehension. Never mind, she didn't need to know that.

"That's a good little kitty," I murmured softly, reaching out for her shiny brown hair, feeling it slipping through my fingers as I stroked it. "A very good little kitty. Now drink your milk."

Her big brown eyes implored me to not make her, but I remained firm. A girl needs to learn to do as she's told, even when it doesn't suit her. Gently I nudged her head, watching even her ears turning redder as the humiliation raged through her, until her pretty face was right next to the saucer, her paws resting either side of it, her little pink tongue creeping out of her mouth.

"Drink it."

I could feel the slippery wetness like a sticky river between my legs, arousal almost choking me as I watched her do as I said. Tentatively at first, then with more enthusiasm, she lapped at the contents of the saucer, with an adorable little cough of surprise when she realized it wasn't milk after all. She looked so subservient, curled up on the floor like that, her hands motionless inside their fluffy black prisons, and I could only imagine how difficult it had been for her to do this. That thought made me glow with desire for her.

Once she had nearly drunk half of it, I reached down and took hold of the pink leather of the collar, tugging on it to motion her upward. Creamy white splashes of the liqueur clung to her lips, dribbling down her chin. Her wide eyes looked up at me, as if waiting for me to ask her to do something even worse. But I didn't. I just stared at her, absorbing every detail of her face, every flicker in her eyes, so close I could smell the sweetness of the chocolate in the liqueur, until I couldn't bear it any longer. Tenderly, I took her chin in my hands and pressed my lips against hers, making her almost gasp, my kiss so light it almost wasn't there. Her eyelids fluttered shut, and she brushed her lips against mine again, as if we were each testing the other, wanting the other to want it as much as we did. And we wanted it so much.

Her tongue pushed between my teeth, parting them until I could feel the coolness of her mouth, taste the sugar and cream and desperate need, my fingers twisting in her hair now, bringing her closer to me. Her body was tense, wanting to reach out and touch me but not being able to, her hands still encased in satin and fur. My poor, helpless little kitten... Just the thought of it made me want to immobilize her more, see her tied up tightly and unable to escape, struggling in her binds as I covered her body with kisses, but I knew this was no place for that. My treasured innocent would have to wait.

"Take me home."

I almost didn't hear her, her voice muffled between my lips that were kissing away the sound of the words. I almost didn't dare hope that was what she had said. But she had.

I pulled away, studying her face, making sure I understood what she meant, smiling back as she smiled up at me.

"Please?"

Who could resist a girl who asked so politely? I stood up to leave, my heart pounding with anticipation, waiting for her to stand up too. She just stayed there, on her hands and knees, looking up at me so beguilingly, waiting for me to lead her. Lead her like a pet, a cherished creature, a purring kitty for me to take. That one moment of offering herself, of taking on her own humiliation without even my request, was the moment I think I fell in love with her. Slowly, so slowly, I walked across the room, not even needing to look behind me to know she was crawling after me, my adoring pet following her mistress to her lair. I waved good-bye to Lynn, whose jaw was almost literally on the floor at the sight of her sweet little neighbor crawling behind me, but none of that mattered now. I waited for my kitten to catch up with me, to crawl to her flat downstairs, where she unlocked the door and wriggled in, letting me follow. I knew I would follow her anywhere.

Her bedroom was just how I expected it, pink and white and girlish and feminine, with cushions scattered across her bed and a teddy bear in the middle. She was waiting for me, curled up on the end of the bed, her back arched, poised for whatever it was I would do to her. Thoughts crossed my mind of how much I wanted to hurt her, to make her cry and beg and scream, then kiss all those screams away, but that didn't seem right for her. No, that would come later. Little kittens don't cry, they purr with pleasure, and lick and stroke and play, and I wanted nothing more right now than to feel that pretty little tongue dancing all over me.

"You *are* a good little kitty, aren't you?" I enthused, rubbing her ears and making her giggle with girlish pleasure. "You don't want to be naughty, though, do you?" She shook her head vigorously, as if it were the most natural thing in the world to be asked such a question, as if she hadn't been standing next to me at a party just a few hours before being taken aback at being asked her own name. "Are you going to show me what a good little girl-pet you are then?" I enquired, getting even wetter just at the thought of it, slowly beginning to unzip my suit, revealing inch after inch of my skin to her. "Are you going to make me come all over your pretty kitty face?"

She looked quite speechless now, her eyes a mix of disbelief and sheer, unadulterated lust, watching as I pulled the zip past my aching cunt and parted my legs for her. I could feel the tightness of the rubber even more now, the coldness of the air making the rest of me feel even more contained in its latex casing, my head spinning with the need to feel her mouth on me. She flexed her body around to reach me, her hands resting either side in their cute little paws, her tongue slowly, unbearably licking the length of me, making me want to scream and grab her head and make her lap at my clit until I came right then and there. But I knew this would be better. This agonizing wait would make me see stars; I just had to endure it first.

She knew this. I could tell from the way her eyes glittered as she looked up at me, the tip of her tongue firm against my clit, circling it so slowly I thought she would almost stop. The cat ears were still perched atop her head, such an irresistible combination of adorably cute and clit-teasingly evil, I knew for certain whatever Lynn had said about her being a "nice girl" was ridiculously unfounded. Or possibly truer than she thought, depending on which way you looked at it.

The flat of her tongue was rubbing languidly against me, my pussy throbbing with a growing warmth as I climbed higher and higher, sparks darting through me, the sensation building almost painfully inside. Just one more flick, one more lick in the right spot, and I would be…I would be…

I came. Waves stronger than I had ever felt before engulfed my body, my wetness splattered across her face as I screamed until my throat felt hoarse. My hips writhed into her, my limbs spasming like I never thought was possible as pleasure jolted through every inch of my being, exhausting me beyond measure. I lay, motionless, unable to speak, as my kitty curled up at my side, planted an affectionate lick on my cheek, then finally spoke.

"So...my slave girl will probably be home soon..." She paused, almost smiling, as if trying to gauge my reaction. "I should go and get her hot chocolate ready for her... You don't mind having two pets for the night, do you?"

I just stared at her, for the first time completely, utterly lost for words. *Well.*

There's certainly nothing quite like nice girls.

SHE NEVER WEARS PERFUME

Sid March

The night is gray; the clouds are charcoal streaks of glitter and snow across an endless urban sky. I am stretched out on my bed, a worn mattress on the crooked wood floor of our apartment on the Plateau Mont-Royal. She is sitting by my feet, trailing her fingers up and down my calves.

She lowers her green eyes and her ballerina lashes project kaleidoscope shadows on her face. She looks so breakable.

"I'm leaving tomorrow," she says, and tugs lightly at the ankles of my black jeans.

"I know."

"Will you miss me?"

"I don't know," I lie.

"I'll miss you."

The air in the room feels so thick. I can barely breathe.

"Christy, I don't want to talk now. I'm tired."

She is wearing too much mascara and four silver rings. I see every last detail. I'm afraid to forget her.

"I'll miss you," she says again.

This is like a monsoon, *la fin du monde*. I stare her down; I change my mind. She can't drown me. I don't blink until she closes the door behind her.

I can't imagine this place if it's not our place. I need to get out. I count the seconds, count her footsteps so I can leave unnoticed. I put on my jacket, my favorite boots, a dark gray scarf. I might blend into the sky.

I slip out the front door, dragging my feet as I walk down our narrow block. I want to drink until tomorrow morning when she will have disappeared, I want to wash away the last few years of my life. There's no point in trying to avoid her. She will never leave without saying good-bye.

I wander down the Main. It's always crowded with the beautiful people, all so young and fashionable, hot women in sky-high stilettos and miniskirts despite the season. I try to expand my chest with a deep breath; I hold my chin a little higher. I try to distract myself. I smile at a slim girl with the most beautiful mocha skin, a tight dress and a tailored men's jacket. Her eyes linger on me a second too long; I taste her pheromones as I pass.

I love those little flashes of *what-if*, but tonight, that kind of charged moment can't even touch me. I consider going to sleep in a snowbank. Instead, I walk toward Carré St-Louis. The snow is piled high around all of the benches except one and a man is occupying the far end. His jacket is dirty and his beard is matted. I sit next to him and stare at the sleeping fountain in the middle of the park.

Gruff-voiced, he mumbles good evening. He's francophone. I return the greeting.

He offers me a drink and a crooked smile. It's a new bottle. I christen it for him and ask his name.

"François."

How perfect. I introduce myself: "Frankie."

His smile gets broader and he asks me why I'm not wearing gloves. Offers me another drink.

I tell him I forgot because my best friend is leaving tomorrow and it has me all fucked up. He says it isn't every day your wife divorces you and I should be there to make sure she doesn't give away our cats.

I tell him I will miss her.

He says she will definitely take the cats. Another man is approaching the bench and François grins and calls out something I can't really understand. I catch his eye and wave goodbye. He tells me if I hurry she might have saved me dinner.

I wonder if his wife had been anything like Christy.

I head off slowly toward the apartment but there's a rock in my stomach, a knot of dread caught in my throat. Blocks later, my key is in the lock. I try to turn it silently. It's dark inside.

"Frankie?" She calls from the front room, her room, where the walls are painted burgundy and the curtains match her bedsheets.

"Christy?" I respond dryly as I head toward the kitchen.

"I really want to say good-bye to you." She is talking a little louder than she ought to, her Maritime accent jangling and frantic, her words clipped short. She's in the hall behind me, but I don't turn around.

"I'm going to have a drink and hit the hay." I throw a few ice cubes into a glass and pour myself a bourbon. Without looking at her, I go into my bedroom, I sigh audibly. I toss my jacket over the chair in the corner.

She knocks at the door. She has such perfect hands.

"I told you I'm going to sleep."

"Please can I come in?"

Another sigh.

I turn the knob and she's standing there with her own glass. Her eyes are shimmering like a blizzard. "Please, Frankie."

Wordlessly, I let her pass. She sits on my bed. I take a heavy swig, put down my drink. I cross my arms over my chest.

"I'm going to miss you so much. Why won't you talk to me?" She stares up at me, almost begging.

"I have nothing left to say."

"I have so much to say to you though; this isn't supposed to change anything."

"Christy, this changes everything." Maybe I'm selfish.

"I wrote you a letter."

I look down at her. Her legs are crossed at the ankle and she's wearing sheer black stockings and a short black skirt. I can see down her shirt. Her bra is red.

"Leave it for me when you go."

"I want to give you something else," she adds and reaches toward me. Her fingers slip into my belt loops.

My heart trips. "What?" I hold my glass tight and put it to my lips.

"Please," she whispers, pulling me toward her. Slowly, I drop to my knees. We are so close I can smell that she is wearing jasmine; she never wears perfume.

I swallow my whiskey and then her mouth is on mine, she tastes like drunken cherries and at first she feels brave; I start to recoil and her soft lips tighten but this is her chance. She puts her hand in my hair; she's pulling the blonde rattail hidden in my short mess of dyed-black. She kisses me again.

"Frankie," she whispers, "I—" she thinks better of it. She starts to unbutton my shirt, tentatively. She looks at me. Her eyes seem unsure, but I can feel that her body is certain.

I don't think we should be doing this, I'm whiskey fueled

and guilt ridden but she's leaving tomorrow; I'm going to miss her so much.

My gaze hardens and my jaw gets tight. Her fingers slip to my belt buckle; she slides it from my jeans and I push close to her; I press her body against the bed. Her hooded eyes flutter.

I rake my fingers down her neck, across the smooth skin of her chest, across the perfect orbs of her full breasts. She sighs and pulls my hair tighter, my face closer to her. I kiss her and she drags her teeth across my lower lip. I glide my hands up the satin of her thighs and press my fingertips hard into the gentle softness of her flesh.

Her tongue probes my mouth and she grabs me by the collar; I reach up her shirt. I am so dangerously close to her heart.

"Frankie," she breathes.

"Please don't say anything," I tell her, sliding off the mattress, my face between her legs. I push her skirt up; her panties match her bra, red lace on gold skin, a perfect frame for her hip bones and the slope of her abdomen. My arm under her hips, I feel like I could take her to the moon. I adore her; I want to rip her apart. I bite into her thighs, carefully at first, then harder and she cries out. I lick my way up, push her panties aside. Slowly, slowly, I trace her with my tongue; her breathing quickens; I paint figure eights on her most delicate parts. I spread her legs farther and slide two fingers inside her. We fall into rhythm; my hand slips into the heat of her wetness, she opens to me, her body bucks. She shakes, I give her more and she pulls at my hair and gasps. Her thighs clench and I wrestle her onto her stomach, press her face into the thin blankets. She is taking my whole fist and I'm wondering how we got here, why she's leaving, but I don't have time, tonight won't last forever, *this is it*. She digs her nails deep into the mattress.

"Frankie," she is almost screaming but I can't listen, "I—"

"Don't talk!" I hurt inside; I want her to hurt; I want her to hurt good. I lift her up to her knees with my hand buried inside her. The light from the kitchen is streaming in and she's glowing lunar. Her skirt is hiked around her waist and I smack the ethereal curve of her ass. My palm makes contact with a blaze of sound, flesh echoing in my pounding head. Again. Again. It's almost cathartic.

She grinds back on me, open to my invasion, to my anger, to my ferocious worship of her body. I see her in slow motion: her shock of dark hair, her flawless skin, the cycling swing of her rounded hips, the tops of her thigh-highs that are starting to slip down her sleek legs.

She slams herself harder onto my fist.

Her breathing is choked out between moans. I grab one of her breasts as I push inside her, then I hold her around the waist; my hand rushes down to give her pleasure; I push my hips toward her. I want her to feel what I feel; I want her to be lost in the throes of ecstasy; I want her to be ravaged by this heartbreak. This is our first night, our last night, our only night. I want her to explode.

She puts her hands against the wall, lifts her hips higher, crying out with every thrust. Her muscles are tightening around my hand, her body falling into frenzy. I'm blind with desire. I run my tongue along her spine; I fuck her in a burst of fury and force her over the edge; she sounds panicked as she comes.

Her aftershocks are like electric tremors. She collapses beneath me and I spread my limbs across hers like I'm hiding her from the world.

"Will you miss me, Frankie?" she murmurs.

"I don't know," I lie.

We don't talk anymore. She falls asleep. I kiss the back of her neck and stare around my room in the dark. I'm awake for what feels like hours, holding her close to me, breathing in the smell of her body, the smell of her perfume, trying to steal every last second with her and lock the moments away for safekeeping. Inevitably, my time runs out and I am lost and dreaming.

When I wake up, she's gone. There's a letter where she'd been sleeping. I don't read it. I won't ever read it.

Christy, je t'aime.

AMATEUR NIGHT

Maggie Morton

Was I really going to do this? Was I really going to dance in front of almost a hundred complete strangers? Yes, they were all queer, so it wasn't like I was adding fuel to the patriarchy machine, or having straight, male eyes leer at me, something I never liked. But I was nervous enough stripping down in front of girlfriends. Not that I had one right now, because I doubt too many women want their partners to strip down to nothing in front of so many people, to dance, to shimmy up and down a pole, and then to give a lap dance to the highest bidder.

Yes, I told myself, I *was* going to do this. Because it was for charity, and because really, what was a little nudity among strangers? It wasn't like hundreds—or thousands—of women didn't do the same thing every day. *It's for charity, it's for charity* would be my mantra.

So I waited backstage, waited my turn, wearing a well-tailored vest and slacks and the sluttiest shoes I could find: Lucite and with much higher heels than I was used to. I'd practiced walking in them at home, noticing how they made my hips wiggle back and forth, how they made me stick out my ass, and especially, how they made me look girly as fuck. And *fuck*, now it was my turn, the femmy DJ calling out, "Next up, we have a lovely lady who goes by the name of Jasmine. Let's give her a warm welcoming. Here's Jasmine!"

That was my cue. I had chosen Marilyn Manson's "I Put a Spell On You" as my song, and as the deep, thudding notes began, I slowly, timidly, walked onstage. The lights were brighter than I had expected, and I could barely make out the crowd, though I could certainly hear them, whooping and catcalling as I began to dance.

I started with a few hip thrusts in time to the music, and then I made my way over to the pole, the music seeming to lead me along, guiding my way, which I hadn't expected to happen. *Fuck*, I thought as I reached the pole. *This is easy!*

Then, as I had planned, practicing in my bedroom, came the part where I'd begin stripping down. That came surprisingly easily, too, because instead of undoing my vest, button by button, I ripped it open as the song grew louder, the buttons flying off, my breasts now completely bare. And I grinned as I heard the crowd's reaction, a loud, boisterous, incredibly positive reaction. Apparently, they approved.

Just before the song got to its loudest part, I got ready: all or nothing now. Yes, I had just shown a bunch of strangers my tits—and loved it. But would I love showing them everything else, too?

Yes, came the answer, as I dropped my pants and strutted out of them, now clad only in a lacy black G-string, my bare, often-complimented ass now revealed. And then a further shock came as I hooked my leg around the pole and spun—once, then twice—arching my back as I did. If the crowd had gone wild before, that sealed the deal. And then, all too soon, the song was over.

Now came the bidding. And then the lap dance, the part I'd been dreading most. Now the only worry I had—no worries about the lap dance, not anymore—was that I wouldn't earn the marriage equality organization enough. Yeah, the crowd had seemed to approve, but still, people could be fickle, couldn't they?

I had no reason to worry, though—two women in the crowd got in a fierce bidding war over me. *Me*! The girl who could barely take off her clothes in front of just one person; the girl who had just stripped down to practically nothing in front of so many people; the girl who had just enjoyed stripping in front of so many people! By the time the bidding ended, my lap dance was going to cost the winner *seven hundred and fifty dollars*. Wow. All that? For me?

I couldn't make her out; the bright lights were still shining in my eyes and when I got down off the stage, it took a few moments to adjust. Thank the goddess, she was cute—shiny black hair pulled back into a ponytail, a curvy figure and a grin that told me, yeah, she was certain she was going to get her money's worth.

"I guess we're supposed to go into the back room, now?" she asked me.

"Yep, that's the plan." So I led this cute, curvy gal into the back room, where she settled onto a small, burgundy couch. I pulled the curtain shut, and now I was ready for my close-up, Ms. DeMille.

The next song started playing in the club's main room—a slow, jazzy number with a female vocalist, her voice rich and sweet. Perfect.

"I've never done one of these before," I told the woman as I approached her.

"Nor have I received one. But based on your performance onstage, I doubt you'll have much trouble." She patted her knee, spreading her legs a little, and the genderfuckery of those two minor actions began to make me wet. Did strippers normally get wet when they gave their patrons lap dances? I didn't know the answer, but in this case, the answer was a very moist *yes!*

I strutted toward her, much more confident, some of said confidence arising from her certainty that I could pull this off—and pull it off fucking well. After all, this woman wouldn't have paid that much if she didn't think I was worth it, would she?

As the singer crooned over the club's loudspeakers, I climbed onto the woman's lap, nothing but a G-string hiding my pussy, and began to grind against her. She bit her lip, and I watched as her eyes scanned me, settling on my breasts for a few seconds, then finding their way down my torso and stopping where our private parts met. I found myself worrying that I might leave a wet stain on her pants, but that worry faded away as I realized I was grinding against something hard, solid and phallic.

"You're packing?" I asked her, giggling a little.

"I almost always pack in public," she replied, grinning at me.

"Well, you get three songs," I told her, and then before I could stop myself, I continued by saying, "and I think that's long enough for a quick fuck."

"Are you...are you serious?" She stared at me, wide eyed, and for a moment, I worried I'd zoomed straight past whatever boundaries she had. I was just about ready to pull my foot out of my mouth and apologize, but then she said, "Lift up a little, I need some room if I'm going to get it out."

So I lifted up onto my feet, watching as she pulled out the dildo I had felt through her slacks. It wasn't huge, but it would certainly get the job done—"the motion of the ocean" and all that being quite true in my experience.

It may not have been big, but I certainly felt it slide inside me, felt it spread me open, felt it especially as she began to move her hips in small, undulating movements. She was writhing like I had up onstage, but this felt even better than the thrill I'd felt as I stripped off my clothes. Yes, it felt far, far better.

"Why don't you fuck me for a while?" she asked. "Why don't you fuck my dick for a bit, cutie?"

"Sure," I said, my voice breathy, and on my knees, I began to rise up and down to the beat of the music; small, controlled movements that brought heat to my cunt, wetness, too, and this woman's dick felt better and better with each movement I made—up, down, it didn't matter, it just felt *good*. And "That... feels...so...fucking...good," was all I could get out of my mouth. We were on to the second song now—it had just begun a few moments ago, but I was already almost ready to burst.

"Get on your knees," the woman told me. "I want to fuck you from behind."

I complied instantly, climbing over her lap and onto the couch. Then I got on my knees, my elbows hanging over the couch's edge. Its back was low, so my own back was almost flat, something that worked to my advantage, because along with the dildo came the woman's fingers, gently rubbing against my asshole, a gentle tease which seemed almost certain to send me over the edge, if only my clit got the tiniest amount of attention. I reached down and began to rub it, the woman's left hand gripping my left hip, her right still teasing my ass. I began to rub faster, somewhat furiously, because the third song had started, and I knew this song, knew it was short, fast, and perfect to get off to. Hell, I'd done that before, a few girlfriends ago—we'd fucked on the living room floor, one of my few acts of kink, and it had gotten kinkier, because she somehow talked me into letting her fuck my ass with our strap-on. It had hurt a little at first, but I had found over the span of just a few minutes that I liked—or possibly loved—how it felt. But there was only that one time, until now. Now I was seconds away from coming. And then I felt the slight pain, and the slight pleasure, of what felt like her pinky's tip sliding inside me, into my ass, and I bit my arm so I wouldn't scream as I came. I found myself fucking her dick as the orgasm took over my body, just like the thrill of stripping had taken me over only three songs ago. This felt better. And the dirtiness, the sheer kinkiness of fucking a stranger after stripping onstage made the throbbing pleasure spreading across my cunt move farther and farther toward an almost godly experience. I hadn't come this hard, since, well…ever? Was this what really did it for me? I wondered about this as my body grew limp. I was spent, even though I was still incredibly turned on, but after an orgasm like that, there's only so much you can do.

And forming complete, intelligible sentences was clearly not part of what was possible for me at the moment. "That's…wow. That was…mmm, yeah. Thanks."

"Good one, huh?" The woman slowly pulled her dick out of me, and I slid the G-string back on. A lot of good that flimsy piece of fabric would do, considering how wet I still was.

"You know," she said, tucking the dildo back into her slacks and zipping them back up, "that's probably the best seven hundred and fifty dollars I've ever spent. I wasn't expecting to get a fuck out of the deal, but I'm certainly not going to ask for my money back. Damn, honey, you're a wildcat in bed."

Now *that* was something I'd never heard before. "Think I should go into this for a living?" I asked her, giggling a little at the thought.

"No, but I would like to suggest your next few hours would

be best spent back at my loft. You know, this isn't my only dildo. I have one that oscillates, one that vibrates, and one that—"

"Eats out whoever's being fucked?"

"Ha! No, I'm afraid not. I take care of that part myself."

"Well, we really should make sure you get your money's worth—and then some. Just let me get my clothes, and I'll meet you outside."

"Oh, you aren't going to go outside like that?"

"I may be brave, brazen, what-have-you, but I'm not crazy." I giggled again, then slowly raised myself back onto my heels, still a little weak from my orgasm. "See you in a bit."

She took my hand before I left, stopping me from leaving. "Name's Miriam, by the way. And is Jasmine your real name? I know you're never supposed to ask strippers that, but thought I'd risk it."

"I'll tell you later," I told her.

But I never did. We fucked for hours that night, back at her place, but right after she drifted off to sleep, I made my exit. Jasmine was just an act, after all. Maybe parts of her would survive after that night—I sure hoped so, and it certainly seemed like they would. A wildcat was awakening inside me. I was ready to let down my hair; to go wild; to scratch, growl, roar and fuck like I never had before.

And no, it wasn't my real name.

CRAVE

Fiona Zedde

Twelve years after Alva left the island, I still dreamed of her. Those dreams were heady and ecstatic, fed by her ambiguously worded letters that gave teasing glimpses of what her American life was like. She told me of the first boy she kissed—she didn't like it—then the first girl who wasn't me, and after that the first time she let someone else touch her in the hidden places that I'd always treasured. I never told her that for me there was no one—no man, no woman—who could take her place in my heart or in my bed. Over the years, the tone of her letters changed. I became an observer of her desires, no longer the object of them. She put distance between us. Soon, my dreams were all I had.

Those dreams were plain, no disguised agendas, no twinned meanings. In the twilight hours, her touch immolated me. It roved with ease over my skin, setting each nerve ending alight, licking my breasts, belly and hips until I arched off the bed, gasping. Many nights I woke with Alva's name on my lips, my fingers buried between my damp thighs, and the phantom smell of her draped over me like silk.

Weeks ago I awoke a few minutes past three a.m. Unable to sleep, I madly scribbled my feelings in a letter to her. At morning's first light, I dropped it in the mail. Afterward, I felt as though I had broken some unspoken rule. Alva never responded. The dreams kept coming and the world itself seemed to conspire to press all its concupiscence on me. Everywhere I looked, people were falling in love and making love. It was in their soft, sighing smiles; the entwined hands, playful touches and ripe laughter as they walked past me in the streets. I even noticed the flush-red hibiscus blossoms with their sticky yellow pistils and moist, inviting insides open to hummingbirds and bees alike. I missed her. I needed her. Then I found out that she was coming.

What the gossips said was that she had been banished back to the island, for lying with American girls. Her mother thought that life back in Jamaica with her father would straighten Alva out. But wasn't she a grown woman, twenty-six, with income of her own like me?

My sisters brought me word that she was coming back, watching my face to see what would show. Did they see my relief? The relaxing of the tension that slid into my body twelve years ago when she flew away from me? I didn't understand then, but I do now. She got the prized passport and the sponsorship of her mother. I didn't, so I had to stay. No amount of crying or bloodied wrists could change that. At fourteen, what did we know about love anyway? But I thought I loved her, thought I would die without her near me. I wondered what she thought now.

The first day that I knew she was mine, Alva and I had left school to play in the park and on the beach nearby. We picked up sweet-fleshed plums from under the trees growing on the path to the water. Under the incandescent heat of the afternoon sun, she shyly pressed the fruit to my mouth and I bit. The temptation was too strong to resist, so I went willingly with her under the canopy of sea grapes where she touched me and rewarded my affections with warm, fruit-flavored kisses. After that, we dreamt together. We planned to leave Morant Bay for Kingston, get jobs in the city and live in a house with plants and a kitchen full of food. We were happy. Then her mother came from New York and took her away from me.

The years passed slowly. With my job at the bank in town I was able to afford my own small place. In it, I luxuriated in the aloneness I'd always craved as a child while crushed in one house between my parents and six siblings. My new home was tiny, four rooms and a little verandah from which I could watch the world go by. Here, no one could see how miserable Alva's absence made me. I wallowed in it, played our old songs and walked to my house, tearing open the shoebox to press her old letters to my face and drown in my memories.

And now she was here. In her father's house, less than a mile down the road. I scrubbed myself in the bath; washed, oiled and braided my hair, and put on fresh underwear. Then I went to her. The house was filled with people, all curious to see what Alva looked like now, to see if she brought something for them from the foreign land. Cousins, friends from basic school, near strangers who walked by her father's yard every day and waved good evening as they passed. They surrounded her, laughing, begging, entranced.

She was perfect: slim and tall, her hair straightened and tucked up in little troughs that rode on her narrow shoulders; skin the soft, teeth-tempting shade of figs and that lush, kissable mouth with the top and bottom lips that were perfect replicas of each other. Not even American MTV could have prepared me for such beauty. Her brown eyes were still quick and laughing, but I did not recognize the hardness around her mouth, the way her hands were still unless she was reaching for something. Those hands of hers used to say so much, chasing the air as she talked, lying open and receptive, pressing against my skin. I hung back, waiting to see if she would notice me, or even realize who I was. I knew that I had changed. I was softer, rounder. My teenaged slimness had disappeared under years of chocolates and bread and fried fish. My mother said that I had become another kind of beautiful. My sisters said I was fat.

In my dreams, Alva had stopped everything for me, brushed all other beggars aside to give coin in the currency of my choosing. But she never looked up, never noticed me standing there with my heart's cup held out. After a half an hour I stumbled away, holding my tears until I walked down the dust-tracked lane where the sun sparkled green and gold on the foliage, mocking my unhappiness. The tears fell freely then. Though rich from the bounty of her new life, Alva had nothing to give me.

That night I made dinner for myself; peeled cassava, yam, and ripe plantains and dropped them in the boiling water. With each movement of the knife I kept seeing her face the last time we were together, the tears that limned its loveliness, the way she had clutched her lip between her teeth as I hovered over her, loving her and crying too. The time for tears was over. I had my life here and she had hers far away. Callaloo and saltfish simmered on the stove, releasing their rich essence into the kitchen. My thoughts of her burned.

I heard a knock at my door. Of course, it was her. She immediately became the most exquisite thing in my house.

"I got your letter." Alva closed the door behind her and

locked it. "I thought you didn't...you couldn't...anymore."

"I never stopped," I said.

A nervous smile came and went on her face. "I missed you."

The words were clumsy on her lips, but welcome. Alva was not as poised as she seemed, and perhaps my palms were not so wet. She lurched forward suddenly and touched me. I flinched, but she was gentle, tracing the bones of my hand with her delicate fingers before reaching for more, shaping my arm, my cheeks, the new roundness of my belly.

"You're gorgeous," she said.

All she'd ever meant to me came rushing back a hundredfold, crashing over my senses until I staggered against her, kissing her. I drowned in the taste of her on my tongue, the silk of her skin against mine. It was too much. I pulled my hand, my self, away, but she followed. Ah, her eyes...I melted, moved toward her, this stranger with the American voice. She caught me up, pressed her cool palms against my cheeks.

"I missed you," she said again.

Kisses like soursop ice cream melted over me, opened me. She was greedy. With her hands and silent mouth she told me what her letters did not, of her hunger for me, her thirst that the twelve-year absence had not dulled. My teeth pierced her lip, she gasped into my mouth and tugged at my dress, determined, but gentle. Her fingers plucked at my nipples, raked them to hardness.

On the stove, the callaloo bubbled and boiled, threatening to eject the pot cover. The strength in her pretty hands always surprised me. They lifted me, threw me on my grandmother's old table. It was sturdy under my weight, solidly straddling the floor as she pushed my thighs open. Her fingers parted the moist hairs under my panties then slid home.

"I'm sorry I made you wait," Alva said.

The fullness of her inside me felt so good that it hurt. Breath boiled in my throat. Soft, needful noises bubbled up in my chest and flooded out of my mouth as I held her close, not quite believing that she was there. Her coconut-scented hair brushed my face and I clenched my thighs around her.

"I should have come back sooner," she breathed. "But I was afraid."

The fingers inside me began to move. In twelve years of lonely nights I had dreamed of this, of her hands on me, the voluptuous wet of her mouth against mine. In a fever, I clutched at her shoulders. My nipples scraped against her shirt, sending electric heat burning through my body. She pushed into me, her breath coming in loud gasps as the table slammed against the wall and my dangling legs jerked in the air. Sweat churned to the surface of my skin, my insides tightened and swelled and my breasts tingled. I grasped at her one last time.

My moans sang out in the tiny kitchen as I twitched and shuddered in orgasm. Alva kissed my mouth and slowly withdrew her fingers. She licked them while I watched, limp from the table. The muscles in my thighs trembled.

"You've always been so effortless," she murmured. "I forgot that too." With quick, impatient motions she shrugged out of her clothes and tossed them on the floor. Almost as an afterthought, she twisted away to turn off the stove. My dinner was already ruined. "Show me your room."

I laid Alva out on my bed and feasted my eyes on the newness of her. The clipped and neat pubic hair, her flat belly and the diamond-studded post threaded through her navel. Her fingers were manicured, cut close and polished a strangely alluring green. I kissed the backs of her hands, then her palms. My smell on her pulled a response, visceral and immediate, from deep in my belly. She smiled up at me from the rumpled sheets, all wet mouth and slumberous eyes. Oh, I missed this, her pliant, pleasure-seeking body under my hands, allowing me to do whatever I wanted.

Her skin smelled of a recent bath and baby powder and sweat. It yielded under my teeth and she moaned softly, arching her neck, widening her thighs. She whispered my name and asked for what she wanted. I slid my fingers against her slick wetness and she groaned, moving her hips against the sheets. The sound of my name on her lips sweetened the air again. I laughed with the pleasure of it and bent my head. She was a stranger to me, someone I had to relearn. I savored the lesson, cupping her soft hips as I charted the delicate geography of her forest and wetlands with my tongue. Hot sensation coursed through my body and pushed my hips against the bed in time to her groaning movements. Alva shuddered against my mouth, whimpering against the sheets as her body undulated and clutched, empty of everything except my love.

I knew she was not staying. How could she? Even now, her body under mine felt transitory, already in flight. Alva shifted until she was the one looking down at me, eyes tracing my face as if to memorize its every curve.

"Are you staying?" I asked.

"No." Her fingers settled on my belly. "But I want you to come with me."

I shook my head. Pain blossomed on my tongue from the fierce pressure of my teeth.

"We can't live here," she said, lacing our fingers together. "Not like this. Not like I want it to be. Come with me."

I closed my eyes. After twelve years, she had finally made my dreams real. How could I give that up? Already my skin clawed itself at the thought of leaving hers. I turned to her in the small bed, the bed that I had bought for us, with one word on my lips.

"Where?"

STELLA LOVES BELLA

V. C. Clark

Two o'clock in the afternoon. I stepped out of the supermarket where I worked and into the real world; in the wet, cold, winter air; snug in my fuzzy black coat; my face hidden by my hood; my world suddenly changed. I forgot about my workday and remembered the reason I'd woken up this morning with ridiculously soaked underwear clinging to my hips and ass with warm sweat, my mind drowned by the images of a goddess.

That goddess is Belladonna. Yes, Belladonna, the porn star; Belladonna, the nastiest *chica* in the adult film industry; Belladonna, the object of my hidden desires. She's the perfect example of the type of woman I want in my life: kinky, filthy, a butt-slut, a lover of ass gapes, a devourer of cunts, the mistress of fetish, the fearless sexual daredevil. She's the kind of woman who doesn't hide her raw sexuality, one who's proud enough to share it not only with her lover, but with the world through the art of pornographic films.

In all honesty, if my girlfriend Mia was a porn star, stripper or exotic dancer, I couldn't handle it. Part of me believes that it's not right to share or sexually expose a lover to strangers. Yet, another side craves the spontaneity, the explicit high, the rush of seeing the one I love doing what she loves best: performing sex, fucking, making love, masturbating; dicks bulging, cum flying, cunts drooling; lesbian orgies, male and female gang bangs... I could go on and on.

I love Mia, but she's not the most sexually adventurous person I've ever known. Hell, she doesn't even like the idea of anal sex, a thing that she knows is my ultimate pleasure. She doesn't understand how I can be aroused by half of the fantasies I've shared with her, some of them involving BDSM, animal training, rope bondage, veggie sex, tit fucking, pussy fisting, and just the simple act of role-playing in costumes—having sex with them on. She finds some of these humorous, the way she finds me humorous.

Mia gave me my first Belladonna DVD for my twenty-fifth birthday. She had no idea who Belladonna was but had heard about her from a friend who recommended the DVDs as a perfect gift. I popped the disc into my laptop and snuggled with Mia on our bed, my eyes glued to the screen.

First scene: a mighty fine dominatrix, reminiscent of Bettie Page, in control of a tied-up, gagged sex slave, teasing her, the naughty pet, and then fucking her with her fingers and then a medium-sized butt plug. I came in my panties, soaking wet; Mia was shocked, not too impressed, her pussy dry. Second scene: simply hot, my mouth watering, my pussy dripping; Mia not getting it, but kissing me, fondling me and licking my ear, acting like she was into it. Scene three: hella good, lots of toys and two hot gorgeous babes, fucking each other S/M style. Scene four: a trillion times better, the best! Belladonna, pregnant, with engorged breasts and round belly, gorgeous, horny, not giving a damn that the belly was in the way of her fucking and being fucked by another girl, the sorority type, the kind I disliked, but *ooh honey*, this chick was a wet dream. Belladonna and the other girl, reacting to their call to ravage each other, pillow fighting, nipple biting, booby sucking, pussy eating, ass fucking; huge dongs plunging in their tight assholes, Belladonna choking on a monster dildo: *Oh, fuck, fuck me Belladonna!*

"Okay, I've had enough," Mia yawned. "It's boring me now."

The end. The best birthday present ever. If only Mia had loved it just as much.

Later in the evening when she was asleep, I watched the rest of the movie. Took out my eleven-inch rabbit vibrator that she despises because it's too fucking huge and so fucking loud. I agree, but dammit, I wanted it. Crammed the bulbous head into my dripping cunt, turned on the bead rotation, the clitoral teaser buzzing, my eyes glued to the computer screen. *Ooh, yeah, that's it*, the fifth and final scene of the movie: Belladonna stuffing humongous anal beads in this woman's asshole—all of them, no holding back. I came; I screamed for more; I got more; I came again. I was convinced: Stella loves Bella. Mia squirmed, shook her head, giggled and muttered, "You weirdo," and went back to sleep. A wonderful finish to a steamy evening.

The next day I ordered three more Belladonna films. More nights of masturbating, fantasizing, yearning, wanting, wandering, dreaming, craving everything Belladonna performed. I realized I wanted a woman like her. It's rare to find a woman open minded enough to explore such filthy fetishes and kinks, desiring the things that I wanted in a fulfilling, daring and adventurous way. I kept telling myself that love was all I needed. But I want more than lovemaking, hand holding, kissing, missionary position, doggy style, shower sex, cuddling, and comfort in loving arms. I want ropes, whips, paddles, cat-o'-nine-tails, leather dresses, vinyl costumes, pony bit gags, ball gags, leather hood masks, wrist cuffs, ankle cuffs, anything and everything outside the vanilla spectrum.

After watching her first movie, I visited Bella's website, becoming a member of her club. I wrote her a letter and sent her pairs of panties in the mail.

One month later, and here I was, walking home with Bella on my mind. The house was empty. There was a pile of mail on the table. I sat down and sifted through the mail. Bills, bills, bills and to my delight, something from Belladonna! She had sent back my panties, beautifully pink. I smelled them—oh! The odor of her cunt! There it was, her autograph, in black ink, oh, Bella! A faded lipstick mark was printed in the center. "Oh fuck, fuck, fuck, Bella, my bitch, I love you!" I cried.

My cunt felt ready to erupt as I hurried upstairs to our room. I closed the door, beads of sweat on my breasts, my nipples protruding through my red dress, knees shaking, wet patch in my panties. I wanted to explode! Still no sign of Mia. Fuck. I needed to masturbate alone without her. *She won't know*, I thought. This was going to be a quickie. I grabbed my silicone butt plug and rabbit vibe, lubing them both up. This time, no Belladonna film. Just a mirror in front of me down below so I could watch as I fucked myself, and of course, my Belladonna souvenir. My asshole and cunt were ready. *Here they cum.* I squeezed the butt plug into my greedy bottom...how easy I swallowed it whole, the base pressed against my buttcheeks, my asshole clenching on it, not letting it go. I rode it, the power to punish, I loved it, watching myself, worshipping my body. My pussy was jealous; I had to give her some love too. I was eager and impatient, no little miss nice girl; I stuffed that humon-gous rabbit vibe deep inside, the clit teaser buzzing against my throbbing pleasure spot. I fucked myself, in and out, hard, pounding, vibrating, earth shattering. In minutes I was gushing with cum. I watched it pour out and slide to the side of my bumcheeks. All the while, my asshole was throbbing, the butt plug a part of my insides, being pushed inside more rapidly by the force of my body. I fucked myself more and more, full speed, sniffing the panties, powerful addictive odor of Bella-cunt, the master of my universe, the mistress of my soul. I could even see her face while I was pounding myself with a vengeance. Bella-donna was mine, I was hers, she fucked me, I fucked her; oh, my, that was the greatest solo fuck session of my life.

I went to the bathroom and washed my playmates with soap and water. Beads of sweat slithered down my back. My dress was soaked with my musky scent. I needed to shower. When I walked out of the bathroom, my sex toys cozy in a towel to be fully dried, I stopped in my tracks. Mia was standing by the bed, next to the pink panties still sitting where I'd left them. She glared at them for a second, picked them up, smirked and stared at me. She looked gorgeous, her dirty blonde hair long and elegant, makeup on her face, prim and proper, Victoria's Secret perfume on her skin, wearing a pink dress with frilly straps, showing off the beautiful curves of her sultry body, purse in one hand, the panties in the other.

"So you finally heard from Belladonna?"

"Yes," I said. I blushed, my fingers shaking, I didn't know why.

"It's sweet that she actually signed it."

She explored the panties with her eyes, trying to find something more.

"Yeah…" I giggled. "Um…I was just going to shower baby, want to join me?"

"Of course, I'm sweating like a pig."

"I love you sweaty." I smiled, walking toward her, putting my bundled towel of sex toys on the bed, shaking, nervous as hell, embracing her. I slid my hands up her dress and cupped her gorgeous, plump asscheeks in my hands, squeezing them gently, my lips against her lips, *mmm*, sweetness, the very thing I wanted, the thing I loved the most, the taste of her tongue, the warmth of her breath, the way she moaned, holding me by the waist, horny thing, trembling over a simple kiss.

"Let's take a bath," she whispered. "I'll get it ready." She went into the bathroom, and started the water running in the tub. I unbundled my towel, quietly putting my toys back in their hidden place. I realized she'd taken the panties with her. I went into the bathroom. Mia was on the toilet, the panties pushed up to her nose, smelling the odor of my Bella.

"I can tell that she sent you more than just an autograph..."

I gulped. Mia's eyes looked devious, sexy, naughty, with the *I am gonna kill you* intensity that I only imagined her letting out in my dreams.

"Oh..." I was speechless.

"Why are you just standing there? Come to me."

Her voice was fiery, demanding control. She grabbed me by the waist, nails pressing into my skin, forcing me down on her lap, my back toward her.

"I can tell that you'd love to be Belladonna's bitch, wouldn't you...?"

She sniffed the panties, her hand grabbing my right breast, squeezing it hard enough to make my nipples instantly pop...it hurt so good. I am usually the master; now suddenly I was weak and Mia was the strong one for the first time.

"Answer me."

"Yes, I do, I admit it..."

"You filthy whore..."

She forced the panties against my nostrils. Oh, that smell, who could resist it?

"In that letter you told her to wear them. These panties are one of your best pair, my favorite actually, and you sent it to the dirty cunt."

"Oh, Mia..."

Her hand cupped my panties, slamming up into me like a hammer to a nail, forcefully. I let out a sharp, puppy-like yelp.

She smacked my pussy, once, twice, three times. Each slap was harder, faster and louder. She bit down on my ear gently, sucking on the lobe and then slithering her tongue deep inside. I melted into a puddle. She tapped my cunt, teasing it, making me squirm with anticipation.

"Fuck, you're so wet Stella. Did you fuck yourself like crazy when you got your panties back from that bitch?"

"Yes..."

With my mouth barely open, she put the panties before my eyes, stretched them out with both her hands and forced them into my mouth. She pulled the sides down hard so that my underwear became a pony-bit gag, perfumed with the scent of Bella-cunt. My moan was loud and helpless.

"Nobody wears my girlfriend's panties but me!" Mia hissed.

She pulled at the ends of the panties as if they were reins and I was the pony. This was unbelievable and beautifully shocking. Was Mia truly jealous? Jealousy made her sexy. I groaned when she pulled the panties harder and tied a knot at the back of my head. The smell, Bella's lipstick mark, and her autograph were crammed into my mouth. My lips trembled. Mia pushed two fingers into my pussy, smooth and easily, pushing the fabric of the panties I was wearing into me as well.

"Do you like that, my little bitch?"

She had her other hand around my neck, choking me for

a second, then letting me go. I breathed loudly and heavily in pleasure; I liked that. She applied pressure again for five seconds then let me go. The sensation was intense.

"M-m-mia...fuck...I love you like this..."

"I can't hear you...you sound like a baby with those panties in your mouth!"

She forced the panties I was wearing into my cum-filled pussy. I screamed.

"Want more?"

With barely a nod, she thrust her fingers up deeper, the fabric of my panties burning my cunt with an intense explosion. I came all over Mia's fingers. She licked my ears, making me weak at the knees. I was trembling and melting. She pulled off my panties, and then slowly crunched bit after bit of my panties inside of my pussy. It hurt like a bitch, the shock and pleasure indescribable. She crammed them all in, letting my panties soak inside my cunt.

"You are so fucking filthy," she growled. "Get in the fucking bath with that dress on." She ripped the panty-gag out of my mouth.

"Are you serious?"

"Do as I say!"

"Yes, Mistress!"

I couldn't believe that I was calling Mia "Mistress." For the first time in our relationship, she was the bitch in charge. I got up slowly, heart pounding, drunk with love, high with sex, pussy panty-stuffed, because of Mia. I turned off the faucet, the tub now full, and stepped in. The water was hot as hell, but oh, how good it was to feel my dress clinging to my skin, the panties in my cunt meshing with my own pussy water, another pleasure that I had never thought of.

"How does it feel?" Mia smirked.

"I never thought I'd ever have panties up my pussy, you bitch."

"It's what you've been waiting for, right? You deserve it."

I was going to reply when Mia bent over and took a Japanese bondage rope out of her purse. Her entire presence had changed; she had stepped into my universe.

She put her feet in the bathtub, fully clothed as well. She grabbed me by the wrists, pulling them behind me, tying them with the rope, nice and tight. How the fuck did she learn such a trick? To my surprise, she lifted my legs up in the air, pressed my ankles to my wrists and tied them together.

"You look so helpless," she said with a scowl. I couldn't move. Mia, so powerful; Mia, so dominant; Mia, my love. She lifted up her dress, revealing a purple, double-strap harness made of vinyl. We didn't own a strap-on, so she must have bought it without my knowing. Then she took out an eight-inch black monster dong, snapping it into the O-ring so quickly and easily, it looked like she'd been doing it her whole life.

"You love being fucked by huge, black dicks don't you?"

"Yes!"

"So big that it will ravage your cunt and asshole to pieces..."

"Oh, god, Mia! I fucking love you!"

She sank into the water and pressed the head of her black dong against my mouth, pushing hard, forcing it in, smacking my face with it. Then she knelt, her dress still on, the water soaking through the fabric. Her warm, slender fingers opened my pussy lips.

"Oh, how lovely your panties look inside of you...I'm surprised that you didn't do this earlier and then send them out to Belladonna."

"I never thought of that..."

She looked at me sharply and dove at my pussy, pulling on

the panties with her teeth. She tugged the entire thing out of me, crammed it in her mouth and sucked the taste of my juices. I threw my head back, grinning, shaking my head, wanting to laugh and thinking that I must be dreaming all this.

"Mmm, you taste amazing," she cooed, tossing the panties to the side. "I'm going to pound you so hard that you won't think about using that rabbit vibrator ever again…"

She grabbed my feet, gripped them tightly and put that enormous dildo into my body.

"Oh, my god!" I roared. She fucked me, her sensually evil eyes stabbing into me, raw and horny, renewed and confident. The bathwater splashed back and forth against my thighs, as she began to pound me at a gentle but increasingly rapid pace. The heat intensified. Mia took me to that place I had always wanted to explore with her: a new world full of daring, raunchy, kinky sex. Mia fucked me better than any man or woman I had ever been with; she knew exactly how to please me and how to ravage me to bits. She squeezed my feet harder—the perfect handles—pounding me faster and faster. I closed my eyes, hearing the panting of her breath, the rush of her intensity, the trembling of her pussy beginning to release. My body ached, the rope felt tighter, chafing my skin.

When she pulled out of me, my pussy clicked and gaped, dripping with my juices. I panted heavily, looking up at my Mia. She growled, grabbed my asscheeks, spread them and inserted the dildo into my asshole. I screamed. The bathwater rushed against my face as she pounded me, hard and rough.

"I love you!" I groaned.

She smacked my face—it was a hot, tingly sensation. I wanted more, and she saw it in my eyes. She slapped my face again and again, stroking my ass. She pushed into me; counted to three, out loud, so that I could hear her; pulled out. She bent over, flicked her tongue around the edge and then dove deep inside, fishing out my orgasms. She teased and played and my cum flowed out of my pussy, dripping into the steamy bathwater.

She grabbed my breasts and squeezed them hard, bit down on my nipples and thrust her fingers into me. She stroked both holes, deeper and deeper, harder and harder. I came a thousand times. She came a thousand times more.

At last she was exhausted, panting and quivering. She collapsed on top of me, the water still warm, washing over both our sweaty bodies and soaking into my rope restraints.

"I didn't know I had that in me," Mia said, hot sweat dripping down her face. "I think this is the naughtiest thing you've ever done, Stella," she whispered. "It really turns me on. Maybe Bella isn't that bad after all."

"She made you into a beast," I breathed heavily, licking her cheek.

"No, you did, honey."

She untied the rope, letting me free. We kissed deeply and passionately, tongues dancing, caressing each other's skin from underwater, as if we were floating in a dream.

"From now on," whispered Mia, "I'm going to be more like Bella. I'll be your nasty bitch."

"Aw, baby doll," I smiled. "You had it in you all along."

She kissed me, her hands traveling to every part of my body, her eyes looking deeply into my soul and taking me to a higher place. Stella will always love Bella. But at the end of the day, Mia is all I'll ever need.

HOMECOMING

Anamika

"Is that Priya Agarwal?"

The voice sounded familiar, but I couldn't immediately tag a name to it. My automatic response was: "I am rather busy right now, could you ring me after some time?"

"Priya, this is Megha Singh, your old classmate from Miranda."

I took a deep breath and my index finger poised on the mouse stiffened. The last I'd heard about Megha from one of my college classmates six years before was that Megha had married a rich hotelier and migrated to the USA. Since we were never on good terms, Megha had not invited me to her well-publicized marriage reception party at a five-star hotel in Delhi where (as one of my friends later reported) caviar was served and a Bollywood item girl was invited to entertain the guests with her acrobatic dancing. Why did Megha call me *now*? I wondered. "Well, Megha, it's nice to hear from you," I said, keeping my voice as cool and courteous as I could manage.

"You didn't expect a call from me, did you?" Megha asked.

"Not really. We were never *that* close, after all." I could have said more, but didn't, fearing that we would end up exchanging some hot words, raking up an unpleasant past that had troubled me in my college days.

"We could meet, you know," Megha said rather plaintively. "I am now in Delhi, staying with my aunt at Vasant Vihar."

"Oh." Even as I made that noncommittal sound, I felt my pulse going up and I felt very hot, even though I was sitting in my air-conditioned office. "I thought you were calling me from your home in New York or is it Chicago?" I said, trying to sound nonchalant.

"Vineet, my husband, is now staying in New Jersey," Megha told me, and then said: "When do we meet, then?"

"Tomorrow, I go to Mumbai for a couple of days to attend a business conference. I will be back on Thursday morning."

"In that case, we can meet on Thursday evening, right?"

Megha's authoritative tone, which had once impressed me, now galled me. So I said: "I will be busy during the week. I am now an assistant manager with Tata Consultancy Service…in case you are wondering why I am not free on Thursday evening."

"I know a little about your present occupation…and also about your single status… Neha told me. In fact, I got your number from her."

So Megha's old confidante and roommate at Miranda had done this little mischief. I would have to warn Neha not to share my personal details with anyone. "I wonder what we will talk about *now*," I said. "Frankly, Megha, I don't fancy reviving a friendship that was never there…if you know what I mean."

"A lot of water has flown down the Yamuna since we met last time, Priya," Megha said. "Maybe we can talk about *that*. How about Saturday evening? You can choose the venue."

Megha was insistent. I took a deep breath, then said: "Seven thirty at Flora, Nehru Place."

"That suits me. Thanks."

It was Neha, my classmate at Miranda College, who had originally introduced me to her pretty, snobbish roommate. Megha came from a rich, conservative and politically influential family in Lucknow. Her family owned a mall and several large estates in and around Lucknow and her father was a cabinet minister in the government of Uttar Pradesh. Apparently, Megha, who studied psychology and was senior to me, was not interested in boys, so Neha thought I could perhaps meet her and find out if she was a "queer" like me. I initially declined to be a part of her dubious project, but when Neha introduced me to Megha and she gave me a tight hug (I fancied she was trying to assess the size of my breasts) and a captivating smile, I was tempted to know her a little more intimately. Neha suggested that a dark auditorium would be the right place for our courtship, so she booked three tickets for a matinee show at Eros, a single-screen cinema, which was showing a mushy Bollywood musical. We sat according to Neha's plan: Megha in the middle and the two of us on either side of her.

The movie theater darkened after the promos, but nothing happened in the first half hour because, experienced as I was in the art of seduction (I had had three lovers—one steady and two casuals—in my senior grade at school), I didn't think it prudent to touch a girl I hardly knew. Neither did Megha show any inclination to take the lead. So, an exasperated Neha, who loved as much to spread news as to create it, volunteered to play the pimp/facilitator: she picked up my left hand (I was after all a leftie), placed it on Megha's right hand and then hissed: "Now start, you dumbos!" I tentatively stroked Megha's long, tapering fingers and then leaning sideways I tried to kiss her, but Megha moved away her face, denying me this privilege. "Sorry, I am not yet ready for *that*," she said.

"You are a pretty girl, Megha, and I like you," I whispered in her ear.

"Thanks, just carry on," Megha whispered back.

I pushed my hand under her top and discovered to my delight that she wore no bra and her boobs were small but firm.

"Please don't rough-handle me, Priya," Megha mumbled and then leaned back. I assured her that I wouldn't do anything to hurt her.

And true to my words I didn't hurt Megha; in fact I handled her body like one handles a newborn baby, stroking and nuzzling her breasts and then sucking her taut nipples. As Megha softly moaned and clutched my hair, I thought we had reached a stage when reciprocation was absolutely necessary. So, I took her hand and slipped it under my top to caress my embarrassingly large boobs. Megha cursorily fondled them a little and then withdrew her hand. I asked her if she was disappointed with my tits. Megha said she just wanted to concentrate on the pleasures I was giving her and didn't want to distract herself by engaging in mutual fondling. At this point, when I was debating in my mind if I should extend my field of exploration below Megha's waist, Neha, the pimp, grabbed my hand, pulled the zipper of Megha's trousers and thrust my hand under her panties. I stiffened, expecting the conservative Megha to evict my eager fingers from her crotch. But she obliged me by spreading her legs. Her smooth, clean-shaven pussy was already swollen, hot and moist, which only showed she was awaiting her spasms. Slowly, I masturbated Megha, stroking her labia with my index and middle fingers and rubbing her clit with my thumb till Megha climaxed, clamping her thighs hard on my wet palm. "Thank you for your good work, Priya," she whispered when I finally withdrew my fingers awash with her cum from her crotch.

"So when are we going to meet again, honey?" I asked her when we came out of the movie theater.

Megha arched her finely drawn brows. "Now, aren't you going a little too fast just after a groping session, Priya?" she said with the superior air of a benefactress who had given alms to a beggar. "I need some time to think about it." And Megha suddenly looked very somber and thoughtful.

I realized belatedly that Megha had used me as a guinea pig to find out what a lesbian couple do to each other when they are left in the dark. I was a fool to let her know that I was besotted with her, and got snubbed for my overture. But unable to banish her from my mind, I buttonholed Neha a few days later to ask her about her roommate.

"Sorry, Priya, she's not going to join your club," Neha said, rolling her eyes. "I told you Megha comes from a rich, conservative family and girls from such families have inhibitions, taboos and whatnot. So forget her and find a new face among the freshers."

"Thanks for your advice," I said tartly, "but I think I can handle my libido pretty well."

Two weeks later, I saw Megha in the college canteen, munching samosas with two of her classmates who knew that I was a "queer." Megha turned away her eyes to avoid meeting my gaze and that irked me. In a moment my thwarted love turned into pure hate and I decided to spoil Megha's reputation as a nice, clean, hetero girl before her friends.

"Honey, you enjoyed what I did to you the other day in the movie theater, didn't you?" I asked Megha, beaming.

"It was okay," Megha said stiffly, looking slightly scared. "Want some samosas?"

"No, thanks. Well, Megha, you have a great body and

I enjoyed fondling you," I chortled, twinkling at her friends' bemused faces.

"You never told us you went on a date with our pussy-loving Priya," one of Megha's friends pouted.

"It was a mistake," Megha said drawing her breath sharply. "You don't really need an extra pair of hands to...pleasure yourself. *That* was not real sex."

"What's real sex, then, sweetie?" I said, pinching her cheek. "And where do you get that?"

A plump girl with braces said: "Wow! What a question! Of course, you need a six-pack alpha male with a reasonably firm dick to give you *that* kind of experience."

Megha blushed and nodded. "Sorry, Priya, Pinky has given you the answer in a bold forthright manner. Now, spare me from your dirty talk on this subject."

Since Megha was not ready for a fight, I did the best possible thing in that situation: I clamped her face between my palms and pressed my lips hard on her mouth for the kiss she had denied me in the movie theater. Her friends twittered and clapped even as Megha struggled to free herself from my grasp. "Some great poet said: 'If there's no help, let's kiss and part.'" I flashed a victor's smile and walked away.

A couple of months later, Neha told me Megha had started dating an athletic boy from St. Stephens, one of the prestigious colleges, and often talked about her ongoing affair.

"Has she done *it*?" I asked Neha, because in those days losing one's virginity was the in thing on the campus.

"Not yet," said Neha, the faithful reporter. "She says she is in no hurry to rush into a physical relationship."

"Good for her," I said. "Because truth could be very unsettling, you know."

"So you think she's one of your kind?"

"I will not say anything right now. Just tell her to watch out before she takes the big leap forward."

"Megha says she's in love," Neha said. "So I would rather wait and watch."

"How is life, honey?" I asked Megha when I ran into her in the college library on a muggy May afternoon. We were in the same aisle and there was no way she could dodge me.

Megha screwed her eyes as if she had seen a dirty beetle trying to crawl up her legs. "You want to know if I have fucked a male, right?" she hissed, her eyes blazing fury.

"Wrong," I said. "I am just curious to know if you have found Mr. Right."

"And how does that concern you? You want to lick my pussy, don't you? You bloody lesbo."

I was quite shocked by Megha's candidness which, I assumed, was her shield against my barbs. Not to lose the war of words, I said: "I also want to kiss your mouth again, and say a few not-so-nice things about you and your sexual preferences."

"Trying to seduce me, huh? Sorry, I am not interested. Look, baby, I am an out-and-out hetero, so stop chasing me. If I ever need a barber to get my pubic area shaved I will certainly give you a call. Now, leave me alone."

"Better call your boyfriend for that dirty job," I shot back, and left her.

The suspense over Megha's painstakingly preserved virginity finally came to an end one morning when Neha confided to me: "*She has done it with Amit, her boyfriend! She says it was an out of the world experience.*" I had a hunch that Megha had asked her roommate to inform me about her plunge into hetero sex to give me a slap on the face.

"Good. Just tell her to practice safe sex," I said.

Neha chuckled. "Don't worry. She carries a packet of flavored KamaSutra condoms in her bag these days."

"Congrats!" I said to Megha when I met her the next day in the corridor.

"So Neha has spilled the beans, huh?" Megha said, beaming. "Spread the word far and wide, if you must."

"What for?" I countered, vexed. "Campus romances are often over with college semesters, so let's talk after six months and we shall see who stands where."

Megha frowned. "If you choose the right partner, romance does not die out in six months or even six years." And with a disdainful smile, she strode away to her psychology class. I felt small and defeated. Maybe I was wrong about Megha. Taut nipples and dribbling pussy couldn't always be the hallmark of lesbianism. Maybe, in the darkened auditorium, her inexperienced body was merely reacting to my clever manipulations. If she had really found love in a male, so be it. Rather than waiting indefinitely for Megha to summon me for some dirty work, I moved away from her path and soon found a contemplative, bespectacled senior girl in the physics department who responded to my advances with suppressed enthusiasm. After the other girls had left the physics lab, we stood behind a rack of optical lenses and smooched and explored each other's bodies and talked about Stephen Hawking.

I had filed Megha as a minor fiasco when Neha, our trusted gazetteer, again brought her into my focus. "Something wrong with her sex life, I guess," Neha confided to me one evening when I ran into her.

"But she looks so proud...and satiated," I said.

"Proud, yes. Satiated, doubtful. She looks rather upset when she returns from that seedy hotel at Kashmiri Gate where Amit takes her every Saturday for sex."

"Look, Neha, no one can satisfy a partner on each encounter," I said. "I read somewhere that premature ejaculation afflicts every male sometimes."

"But she says he stays firm for more than five minutes," Neha reported faithfully.

"Then she's frigid." And I couldn't help remembering the copious tears of joy her pussy had shed in my palm in the movie theater.

"You may be right, Priya," Neha said. "At least on two occasions I have noticed that after she returned, she sneaked into the toilet to masturbate."

"Tell her to see a shrink or a sexologist to improve her sex life," I advised Neha glibly.

The last time I saw Megha before she vanished from the campus was in the college lawns, munching peanuts desolately. I didn't want to talk to her, but she called out: "Hey, Priya, going to hump that morose zombie in the physics lab?"

"Right you are, babe," I said cheerily. "At least we don't come back to our rooms with dry vaginas and rush to the toilet to do some hard work with our fingers."

"Sneaky bitch!" she growled. "I will throw Neha out of my room one day."

"But that's not going to help you to achieve what you are missing," I teased.

"Fuck you, you bitch!" Megha hissed.

"Fuck you, my love," I cooed.

And that was how we parted.

Two months later Megha dropped out of college to marry,

not her athletic lover Amit, but a potbellied restaurateur who owned a chain of Indian eateries in the USA. "Money is very important for Megha's folks, I reckon," Neha told me. "And Megha went for it."

"So, how is life, Priya?" said Megha, as we sat at a corner table of Flora. The restaurant was crowded on Saturday evening and we had to wait to get our table.

"I am fine," I said. "You are on a vacation, I suppose?"

"No, I will be here for a while."

"Ah." I looked at her and she looked at me, perhaps both wondering how life had treated us in the last six years. Megha looked subdued and her dress was sober, if not shabby—frayed jeans and a beige top that didn't flatter her curves. Her shoulder-length hair looked unkempt. I guessed that she was going through a bad patch. I also noted that she had no wedding ring. *A divorcée?* I wondered and the evil spirit that resided in me chuckled with glee. Denying one's natural inclinations could lead to disastrous compromises. "How about a soft drink?" I asked.

"I would prefer a hard one—if you don't mind," Megha said, stealing a glance at the bar at the other end of the restaurant.

"A gin and tonic?"

"Scotch with soda and ice will be fine."

So I beckoned a waiter and ordered single malt, large, for Megha and a Pepsi for myself.

"You don't drink, I assume," Megha said, watching me with some curiosity.

"I drink a cocktail or two when I attend business parties." I wondered how long Megha would continue this small talk. Or was she here just to check out how I, her one-time *bête noire*, had fared in my life? Megha kept up the small talk till our drinks were served and she had taken a couple of sips of scotch.

"You look good, Priya," she said scanning my face and the visible upper half of my body that included my much-ogled big tits.

"Thanks," I said, with a wooden smile. "One has to dress up and put on a little makeup too to look good and professional in my line of business."

"You must be wondering what I am doing here in Delhi in this muggy weather when I am supposed to be with my husband in New Jersey, changing nappies or reading bedtime stories to my kids," she finally began.

"I guess you are separated or have divorced and have returned home to lick your wounds," I said looking straight at her face.

Megha smiled wanly. "You have sharp eyes, Priya, and I appreciate that. You have always been a good observer, I remember."

"Thanks, Megha, but I still don't have any idea what prompted you to seek me out, particularly when we are not and have never been on the same wavelength."

Megha sighed. "I thought now that I am back and...well most of my old mates have married and settled down with their own families, kids and whatnot, you could be the one with whom I may perhaps spend an evening or two without talking about my disastrous marriage."

I felt a strong urge to tell Megha that I led a pretty busy life and had no time to spare for her. But I checked myself. Megha took a long sip of whisky and then did something for which I was not prepared at all: she grabbed my free right hand and pressed my fingers to her wet lips. That was the moment when I realized that even after all these years I still fancied this woman.

* * *

"I knew I was treading the wrong path even as I courted Amit, that St. Stephens hunk," said Megha, as she undressed in my bedroom. I sat regally on the sofa and watched her shedding her clothes, my nipples already hardening. Megha hadn't gained weight, I noticed. She still had a supple body and firm breasts.

"I am not interested in your past, Megha," I said, watching her unbuttoning her jeans.

"I must tell you why I spurned your advances in those days," she continued. "Look, Priya, I came from a conservative family where men make all major decisions and marriage is just one of them. My dad is in politics; he is still a minister in the state government of Uttar Pradesh. I had to suppress my sexual urges because even a small family scandal could jeopardize my dad's career. If I had tried to wriggle out of the closet, told him that I didn't want to marry a guy, he wouldn't have hesitated to kill his only daughter. That's how our patriarchal society behaves in my part of the world."

"I understand," I said. "I guess you suffered a lot in your forced marriage with the rich hotelier."

"It was terrible," Megha said, wriggling out of her panties. She hadn't clipped her pubic hair for a while, I noted. "Vineet turned out to be a pervert. A keen watcher of blue films, he subjected me to all sorts of kinky sex. It was disgusting. To avoid pregnancy, I took contraceptive pills on the sly. When he discovered this, he burnt my crotch with cigarette butts and then threw me out of his house."

"I am really sorry for you, Megha," I said. "You must try to forget your past and start life afresh."

"And for that I need help from my old friends, particularly from you. I treated you so badly in those days that merely asking your forgiveness now…"

"...Won't work," I cut in. "You deserve punishment and you will have it. Come to me, bad girl."

Megha smiled wanly, wiping the tears that had gathered in her eyes, and then approached me like a chastised schoolgirl, her tits jiggling and her bird's-nest bush lightly brushing my shoulder. I drew her onto my lap, turned her over and then slapped her bum hard a couple of times. Having delivered the punishment, I pressed my mouth fiercely on hers, savoring those well-curved lips that she had denied me when we were at Miranda. I explored her mouth with my tongue and then nuzzled her breasts. As Megha started kneading my boobs, I stood up from the sofa, lifting her in my arms. It was pure, simple lust that gripped me. I hadn't had sex for over a year now and here my elusive lover of yesteryear had turned up. I dumped her on my bed and then, tearing off my skirt and blouse, I spread her legs wide and ground my pussy vigorously against hers. She moaned with pleasure but her luxuriant bush denied me the pleasure of rubbing my wet pussy against her naked flesh. So, I finally dived between her legs to suck her labia, lick her clit and then finger-fuck her, making her groan, arch her back high and then shriek as the orgasm finally hit her.

We ended up kissing each other, our busy fingers exploring each other's bodies. We hardly spoke for we were actually preparing ourselves for an encore.

Late in the evening, when an exhausted Megha took leave of me, she asked: "Seems you are still without a partner. Would you mind if I come to live with you on weekends?"

"You are welcome, hon," I said. "But do come with a clean crotch or I will have to hire a barber to clean up the mess."

POOL PARTY

Zoe Amos

It was one of those days when the heat slows you down and the humidity curls the wallpaper off the walls. There's not much to do on a Sunday after church in a sleepy Southern town in the middle of August except try to stay cool.

Michelle envied her neighbors with backyard pools. She wiped her bandana across her forehead and rolled it up to make a headband. She knotted it in place behind her head where it got caught in the frizz of her hair. The thought of buying a Walmart kiddie pool was tempting, and she snickered at the idea of filling it up in the middle of her apartment. At least her feet would stay cool. Right now, the only thing she had was a rapidly warming can of beer propped between her legs as she sat on the balcony of her second-story apartment looking across the parking lot at the back of Jenkins' Hardware. The aluminum can did little to temper the heat radiating from that part of her body. There was only one cure for that, and she hadn't seen any action since LaTanya said good-bye.

LaTanya had a small above-ground pool at the house she rented and they'd used it a couple of times shortly after they met last September. That option was out of the question since they'd broken up in May. LaTanya told Michelle not to call until she developed the part of her brain that controlled common sense, which would probably not come this century judging by her lack of judgment and unacceptable behavior. It was over with a capital O and Michelle knew why. Her dalliance with the girl from Ole Miss who was home on Spring Break had cost her the relationship, a fair price to pay. When asked by her (ex) girl-friend to explain why she felt compelled to diddle around like that when she already had a perfectly good relationship going, Michelle didn't have an answer. That was the end of that and there would be no more fun and splashing around in the long hot days of summer.

Through the grapevine, Michelle heard that LaTanya was taking a break from romance by putting her energy into her job at the cable company. Just what the world needed: another crabby customer service rep. The misadventure was three months ago, long enough for the anger to have settled and for her to try again. Yes, LaTanya could be full of attitude, a bitch some might even say. Not always. There were plenty of fun times, and a little fun in the pool with its sparkling water would be a great way to get reacquainted. The idea of cooling off and the prospect of a rekindled romance took over Michelle's mind. She finished her beer, got in her pickup and drove to LaTanya's without calling first.

Once she was past town, the dusty road was empty of cars. Traversing the long driveway to LaTanya's house, she knew anyone home would spot a visitor long before they reached the front door. LaTanya's SUV was parked by the side of the house not far from a silver Honda Civic. Michelle swung her pickup in a half circle and parked. Dust rose up beyond the window and stuck to the sweat on her forearm. She checked her appearance in the rearview. It wouldn't have been a bad idea to spruce up a bit before arriving, but now it was too late. She walked up to the front porch. Buddy, a golden retriever, was sprawled in the shade next to a metal chair with no cushion. He flapped his tail against the floor without lifting his head.

"Hey, Buddy. Remember me? I think you do. Hot one, ain't it? No, don't get up." She rapped her knuckles on the screen door and looked inside. It was likely LaTanya was in the pool with her housemate, Deni. She walked around to the backyard. The pool water sparkled in the sunlight, just as she remembered. The pool was empty save for a floating beach ball.

"Anybody home?" she called out. "LaTanya?"

The back door slammed shut. "Michelle. Hey, haven't seen you in an age!" It was Savannah, LaTanya's younger sister. Her hair was wet, as if she'd just gotten out of the pool and gotten dressed. Her shirt clung to her in a way that reminded Michelle of LaTanya when she'd first seen her at her own job, stocking cans at Winn-Dixie.

"Hey, yourself. Thought I'd pay a call. Is LaTanya home? Her car's here."

"No, I drove her to the bus this morning. She's gone to Atlanta for a few days of training. I'm house-sitting and taking care of Buddy."

"Where's Deni?"

"She moved to Tallahassee. Didn't you hear? She got a scholarship."

"You don't say. She was a smart one. Got out of here when she could."

"I bought her Honda. Now I've got me some wheels." Savannah smiled and raised her eyebrows in delight.

Savannah looked like a younger version of LaTanya, and Michelle caught herself staring at her. She shifted her gaze to where a mature pecan tree shaded part of the yard and the edge of the pool. Next to it was a lounge chair with a towel draped over the back and a small table holding a colorful tumbler.

"Would you like a glass of tea?" asked Savannah. "I was about to get a refill."

"Thanks. That'd be nice."

Michelle watched as Savannah retrieved her empty glass. The long grass brushed against the girl's ankles. Her movements were springy, and the combination reminded her of an antelope bounding through a glade. Her body exuded a freshness Michelle found attractive.

"If you don't mind my saying," Michelle said, "you're awfully light on your feet for such a hot day."

"I just got out of the pool. You should go in."

"I'd love to!" Michelle grinned and stopped herself from touching Savannah's bronzed arm. "I didn't bring a suit. And I don't have a towel."

"Just go in. Haven't you ever skinny-dipped?"

"No."

Savannah put her hands on her hips. "Well, then it's about time. Nothing feels better than being in the water nekkid. I only wear my swimsuit because LaTanya and Deni do, and they're not here. Try it! You'll never want to wear a suit again. I'll go in with you."

Savannah brought out their ice-filled drinks and a fresh towel for Michelle. They had a few sips of tea and made small talk. Savannah talked about her latest doings and classes coming up at the community college, but Michelle didn't have much to add—she had the same job, same apartment, same life.

"You should take a class this coming semester," said

Savannah. "You're good on the computer. You should go for your certificate."

Michelle nodded. She was up for something new.

Savannah set down her drink and retied the rubber band holding her hair. "Ready?" she said, gesturing toward the pool. "Just go for it. Don't worry. The nearest neighbor is a quarter mile off." Savannah stood in front of Michelle and stripped off her top, followed by her shorts and underwear. She casually dropped her clothing on the lounge and stood "nekkid."

"Now, you."

Michelle gave Savannah a wide-eyed once-over. How could she not? Her lithe, young body with its enticing curves was there to be noticed. Without apparent offense at being ogled, Savannah climbed the pool ladder and Michelle watched as Savannah's shapely butt edged into the water.

The pool was four feet deep with the sides a little higher. It was aqua blue with stiff white side supports that made it seem like a circus pool, the kind high divers drop into from the uppermost reaches of the big top. Savannah stretched out and glided over the water into the pool's center.

"Come on, now. Don't be shy." She batted the striped beach ball toward the ladder. "We'll have ourselves a private pool party."

Moist from the heat, Michelle's sticky body grabbed at her clothes as she rolled them over her arms and legs. As the little hairs on her skin detected a slight breeze, she felt cooler. She could especially feel how hot her pussy had become underneath her shorts. She liked the feeling of air against places that rarely remained unclothed and while she thought it would be pleasant to enjoy the sensation a little longer, she reached for the pool ladder.

Her foot touched the water on the inside of the pool and

registered a perfect temperature. It wasn't like the public pool. If there was chlorine, she couldn't smell it, and she dropped her body in.

"I feel like nature girl!" exclaimed Michelle. She laughed as the water tickled past her privates, over her stomach and washed away the line of sweat beneath her breasts. "I can feel my skin."

"That's what makes skinny-dipping so much fun!"

Savannah draped her arms over the edge of the pool while Michelle swam in a circle.

"I know a fun game," said Savannah. "Take your do-rag and put it over your eyes. Then try to tag me. You say 'Marco' and then I say 'Polo' so you can hear where I'm at, but I'm going to try to fool you and sneak around. Okay?"

"I know that game." Michelle dipped her bandana in the water and squeezed it out before placing it over her eyes. Savannah swam off and after Michelle tagged her, they switched roles. On the second round, Savannah tagged Michelle's foot while trying to escape. Savannah took off the blindfold and handed it back.

"I have a boyfriend," Savannah said. "Junior Peyroux."

"That's nice," Michelle said.

"We do it."

Michelle hummed knowingly. Savannah wasn't a kid anymore.

"You know what he does?"

"Well, I can guess," Michelle said. "Are you sure you want to tell me?"

"I'd rather show you." Savannah bobbed in the water closer to Michelle. "I mean, on me." Savannah held her own nipples between her thumb and forefinger and gave them a twist. "See what happens there? Takes two secs and they're standing up like nobody's business. But it hurts! Did you ever do that to LaTanya?" Savannah's tits were perky and higher than the water line where Michelle had an eyeful.

"No. Savannah, that's kind of private."

"The reason I ask, is I don't have much experience. Junior's not my first, but unless I know what to do to fix things, I'm ready to drop him. Show me, Michelle. Show me what to do so I can tell him."

"You want me to show you?"

"Touch my breasts the right way. Please! I promise I won't tell a soul you showed me, not LaTanya or Junior or anybody. I have to show Junior what to do." Savannah took one of Michelle's hands and placed it on her breast.

Michelle let her hand drop into the water. It was a simple response and a hard one to make. "I don't know. I shouldn't." Savannah looked mighty good with her nipples twisting into hard points. Opportunity was knocking, begging for her to open the door...but this was LaTanya's little sister. If she hoped to ever put something back together with LaTanya, she had enough common sense to know this wasn't the way to do it.

"Then you tell me what feels good." Savannah would not be stopped. She placed both her hands on Michelle's large breasts beneath the water and pushed them together and apart in a circular motion. "Is this good?"

"Savannah, really now! Well, yes, it feels good." The turn of events was not a bad thing. After all, she had no guarantee LaTanya would take her back. She was feeling much refreshed from the pool and now LaTanya's hot little sister was insistent. How could she refuse? "This is to help you with Junior, right?"

"Yes. Please say you'll show me."

"Okay, I'll show you."

Savannah dropped her hands and stood a little straighter as

if to demonstrate she was ready, showing off her pert breasts as they floated at the water line.

"Um, usually I'm kissing a little before going there…"

"Then we should kiss. You can never have too much practice," Savannah declared as she put her arms around Michelle's neck and brought her lips near. "Go ahead. Kiss me. I know you kiss girls all the time."

Michelle embraced Savannah around the curve of her waist and looked into her eyes, warm and brown, her lashes wet and stuck together in dark, shiny spikes. She closed her eyes and kissed Savannah gently, not sure if she should open her mouth. Michelle kissed the young woman's face and landed back on her lips while naturally moving her hands, squeezing her close. Her breasts felt good against Savannah's chest. Savannah opened her mouth slightly and Michelle licked inside then came out and sucked on Savannah's generous lips. She moved her hands slowly to the front and positioned Savannah to delicately massage her tit, being careful not to focus too much on her crinkled nipple. Her hand squeaked along the wet skin. She broke from their kiss and looked at Savannah.

"That's what I'm talking about—feeling right nice. Junior never did anything like that. He's always acting like he's in a hurry, like his daddy is going to walk in on us any minute."

"Well, forget Junior for today," Michelle said as she dribbled a stream of water from her hand down Savannah's front. The water trickled into separate rivulets and fell back into the pool.

"Aren't you going to finish?"

"More? How many lessons were you thinking?"

Savannah put her finger on Michelle's lower lip and Michelle took the tip into her mouth and suckled it. "I'm thinking we should at least finish what we started."

"You want everything? Like…" Michelle nodded her head

at everything below the waterline. Savannah nodded. Michelle smiled. This was her lucky day. "Then we best get out of the pool. Water's fun for some things and better when you're more experienced. I think we should get out."

They climbed out and toweled off. Their tea had the last traces of ice and was getting warm, but its sweet wetness was welcome nonetheless. Savannah suggested they lay their towels side by side beneath the pecan tree, as it would still be too hot in the house. Savannah lay down on her back. Her breasts perked skyward and her bush began to dry into a small, unruly ball of fluff. Michelle joined her and the two made out beneath the shady branches. Savannah tasted of sweet tea and her face and neck were salty with perspiration.

Michelle took her time loving the young lady. Savannah was receptive to her touch and let it show. Michelle traced her fingers up and down Savannah's firm curves. She made circles around her breasts, winding in smaller and smaller spirals until her fingertips found their center point and stayed there. She pressed in each nipple and then moved up and down Savannah's body with licks and kisses until she landed on first one nipple and then the other, mindful of avoiding anything that might be rough, and certainly doing nothing like what Junior might have done in the name of lovemaking. Savannah hummed a sigh-like note from time to time and didn't seem the least bit self-conscious or timid as she experienced Michelle's touch.

"You want everything, huh?" Michelle asked. Savannah's reply was to open her legs. *This is too good to be true*, thought Michelle, *and yet, here we are*. She ran her fingers the full length of Savannah's body. The young woman flinched when her toes got tickled. Savannah laughed.

"Is it okay to laugh while you're doing it?" she asked.

"Sure! Ain't nothing wrong with that. Just have yourself a good time." Michelle resumed her massage and Savannah let out a little moan. "See, this is better, isn't it?"

"Oh, yeah. I was thinking what to do about Junior when you pulled up the drive. And I thought to myself, who's going to know more about what a woman likes than a woman who knows what other women like?"

Michelle chuckled. "I'm glad my reputation is good for something."

Savannah opened her legs a little wider and Michelle made her way down, stopping to lick the moisture pooled in Savannah's navel. She blew onto Savannah's bush to separate the hairs and saw a little pink skin hiding inside. Parting the hairs with her fingers, she could see a slight glistening. She reached both of her hands beneath Savannah's butt and raised her up to her mouth. She kissed and licked high up on both sides of her legs before settling into the wet center of her youthful womanhood. Again, Michelle took her time, a fact Savannah seemed to appreciate. No one's daddy was going to interrupt them. Her tongue ran over and around, inside and out; she suckled and kissed and tried to think of ways to give pleasure, ways that were most likely new and wonderful judging by the hardened nub nestled beneath the younger woman's mound.

Without warning, Savannah bucked up as if her butt had caught fire. "Oh! Oh! That's it! Oh!" Michelle released her hands and let Savannah's bottom rest on the towel. "You did it! I did it!" she cried. "I finally had an orgasm! Wow!"

"You never had an orgasm?"

"Nope." Savannah looked sheepish. "Never did. Until now, that is."

"Well, hallelujah!"

"It was incredible! Like I'm shivering from the inside out.

But...I was hoping you'd, you know, with your fingers. And now it's over."

"We can still do that," Michelle said.

Savannah sat up wide awake. "Really? But I already..."

"That's okay. We just keep doing it, that's all. Since this was your first, take a little break and enjoy the feeling." Michelle nudged Savannah back onto the towel and gave her a little body massage to keep her interested. After a few minutes, she positioned her leg between Savannah's and pressed in over and over with her firm thigh. Then, she moved her hand down to Savannah's fuzzy bush. She licked a finger—not that she needed to—and held Savannah on her nub for a few moments without moving. They kissed and Michelle rocked her finger a little at a time until it had entered its mark. She kissed Savannah's neck as she worked her down below. It was a challenge to stay focused and not think about coming. Her own twat, which pulsed and dripped pussy juice down her leg, was becoming as insistent as Savannah. Michelle finger-fucked her for a good, long while, and with one thrust, Savannah announced to everything within a mile her unbelievable pleasure. Michelle's fingers were squeezed so tight she thought the circulation would quit. And then Savannah shuddered and fell on her back, exhausted, catching her breath.

"Holy Christmas! I had another one! So this is what you and LaTanya were up to."

Michelle pressed on her own clit. The pressure had gotten almost painful and she could feel it throbbing. It wouldn't take much for her to come. "Not exactly," she replied while trying to even out her breathing. "It's different; with everyone it's different. You were amazing."

Savannah propped herself up on her elbows. Her dark body gleamed as dappled sunlight danced around across her skin. She glanced at Michelle's hand, which seemed frozen with tension. "And then did LaTanya take a turn with you?"

"Sometimes we took turns and sometimes we did it together. I know I could use a little help right about now. This has gotten me all worked up. In a good way, mind you. But you don't have to. I can do it."

"No, I want to! Let me. Lie down. Right here." She patted the ground, sat up and made a space on the towels for Michelle. "I probably won't be as good as you. I've never done this—to myself. I told all my girlfriends I did, but that was only because they said they did it. Really, I never have."

"Are you sure you want to?" asked Michelle.

"It was better than I ever imagined. Like a triple rainbow, and peach ice cream, and all my favorite things in the world. Now I know what everyone's talking about. I want to try. Let me try." Savannah's eyebrows arched upward in a nuanced gesture, the same pleading Michelle saw earlier in the pool, and she knew she could not refuse.

Savannah was a good student. She imitated some of the things Michelle had done and made her wait. Michelle was fit to be tied by the time Savannah got around to pushing in one of her fingers. Michelle came instantly. And being a good student, Savannah had also learned that unlike her experiences with Junior, coming didn't mean stopping. By the time they finished with each other, the sun had lowered in the sky and the unbearable heat had slackened. They took one last dip in the pool, splashed around and embraced in the cool water. Buddy wandered by with his food dish in his mouth, and dropped it by the lounge chair. He let out a shrill yawn and looked up at Savannah expectantly.

"Someone's hungry, huh, Buddy?" Savannah said. "Guess it's time to get out."

After they dressed, Michelle embraced Savannah again and kissed her deeply with her tongue. She looked into her dark brown eyes. "Now you promised not to tell and I'm going to hold you to it. This here's a small town and I'll find out if you do."

"What's to tell?" said Savannah. "That Junior and I broke up and now I'm going out with you? What do you suppose folks would say about that?"

Michelle smiled and kissed Savannah on the forehead. "They'd say, 'I never did understand why a smart girl like Savannah was hanging out with that Peyroux boy.' And I'd have to agree."

DAFFODILS

Sally Bellerose

I am vainly, passionately in love with my garden. I consider each crocus bud to be swelling by the grace of the sweat that dripped off my neck while I planted last fall. The curves of the tulip leaves are the curve of my back, straining with the pitchfork over the compost heap. I have an ex-lover, Annie. My old girl-friend appreciates my vanities. She's a fecund woman of fifty-five. Fecundity. God, I love that word. A word that celebrates the muck and mire we all spring from, the richness of life. A word you can use without feeling corny about the filling, swelling, bursting going on inside and outside of you.

Like everything else in nature that's alive and kicking, my ex-girlfriend and I know a sexy season when we feel it. Spring is fucking time. Since we broke up, there have been some years when I don't see Annie all winter long. But you can bet your last tube of Vagilube, she's going to show up at my front door, sometime before the season begins and as sure as taxes are due, smiling like she never ever did one wrong thing. She's the first sign of spring: soft, moist and furrowed.

This year Annie came on April first, All Fools' Day. I know because my present, love-her-madly-till-death-do-we-part, girlfriend left for a conference in Erie, PA that morning. My girlfriend's tracks where still fresh on the driveway when *knock, knock, knock*, Annie's at my door.

We sit quietly in the living room. I pour coffee. Her body, full on my couch, extravagant, is what my grandmother would have called pleasingly plump. In fact, Annie looks a lot like my grandmother, except her hair is not gray. Annie dyes her hair red; not auburn, *red*. She looks incredible. It's one of those days when the light is so bright and the air is so clean that everything seems possible. I look out the window. I see my neighbor's rusty trash cans on their sides near the border of my garden. The damned kids have thrown them over the fence again. When I smile at the sun bouncing off the dirty metal barrels, I know Annie and I are going to end up naked.

It's always the same. We start out polite, acting like we aren't affected by the bulge in the daffodils anymore, pretending we don't have some unspoken pact to celebrate the rituals of spring together, year after year. We're dying to find out what changes and what remains the same, but we start out slow, just in case one of us has decided that we should quit while we're ahead.

Annie and I were born the same year in the month of April. We met in the spring, twenty-two years after our separate births. We were young together. We were young together until we were forty-six. Then we weren't together and we weren't young. Middle age: I've never been able to wrap my mind around that season of life. It's not what I expected. I thought middle-life would take over and make me respectable, settled, comfortably bored. Now Annie and I are both fifty-five, on the cusp of old age, approaching old-ladyhood as unsettled and wanton as we were thirty-three years ago. Annie says you're only as old as you feel. Well I feel fifty-five springs horny.

I look at Annie, wrinkles deepening around her eyes as she smiles at me. I see old familiar lust forming in the lines at the corners of her mouth. She brings her coffee to her lips. There's a fold inside her elbow that I don't remember from last year. *Annie, we're turning into old women with desire tucked in the bends and kinks of our skin.*

Old women, I like the sound of that. I touch my neck, my skin warm and loose. Old women, sitting on the couch unfolding. I like the feel of it. Especially in spring. Spring has a way of honoring the layers of life that came before. The thicker the blanket of dead leaves, kitchen scraps, manure and snow, the more succulent the hyacinth's new shoots. I like having all those winters, all those springs backing me up. It's good that I'm still alive. I'm just starting to get the hang of life. It's mostly the dying at the end part I'm having a hard time adjusting to.

I lean back on the couch and close my eyes. Annie sits quietly beside me. She touches my hand. Softly her fingertips turn over my memory. I think of Annie's hot breath on the back of my neck, her fingers reaching around my waist to unzip my jeans from behind. I don't think of us as any age. I remember how the sweat forms in the small of her back as she moves on top of me and calls my name. I try to remember where we found the guts to take these liberties so long ago. Even youth doesn't give two women license to do these things together. Maybe age stops asking for permission.

I open my eyes and smile at Annie. The older I get, the better my long-term memory gets and I can't remember Annie ever asking for permission to do anything. Maybe she was old before her time. She never asked me if she could sleep with other women when we were together. We had a deal. We were doing the "don't ask, don't tell" thing long before the military.

But sleeping with other women wasn't why we broke up. Our deal worked out fine for the most part. It was good we broke up. It was getting so we weren't being nice to each other on a day-to-day, everyday schedule. It was time to go our separate ways. So we did.

"Let's see the garden," Annie says.

We walk out to the yard. We gossip among the crocuses. They're in bloom, tiny things, only six inches from the ground, but they're full of themselves, screaming yellow and purple. The first to flower, brave little darlings. There's a chill in the morning air. Still, you can feel it's going to be a warm day. The ground is damp. It feels nice to sink into each step just a little as we walk. Annie compliments my tulips, marvels at how many there are, more than last year, more than the year before. They're all up, awake, out of the ground, seven or eight inches high. The leaves are striated green and rusty red, profuse and pushing. They're not ready to bloom. They have maybe a foot more to grow and gallons of sun to drink.

It's the daffodils that grab us, stop us in our tracks. We stare for a full minute before we walk toward them, our mugs of coffee steaming in our hands. The daffodils are swollen, not one bloom actually open among one hundred. They're straining. They want to get *on* with it, bad. They're tired of waiting. You can feel their impatience, just a little more time, just a little more light, a little more sun. Something inside them is pushing. *Open.* This is the time. *Open.* This is the place. No shame. They stand in clumps, leaves turning toward the sun. If it were rain, they'd be just as ready. They know who they are, what they want.

Annie and I stare at each other and sip. Annie presses the warm mug to her cheek. The coffee steam rises. I brush my own cheek against my own cup and stare at Annie. It's the morning sun, it's the season, it's me that makes Annie's face glow, but it's something else, too. Annie's happy. She's happier than I've seen her in a long time. She's in love, not with me. She has a new lover. I'm not guessing. I've met the woman. Nice woman. She makes Annie happy. I wonder what kind of deal Annie has with her new lover. I don't ask. Annie doesn't tell.

I push Annie's new lover out of my mind. I push my own lover as far out of my mind as she will go: Erie, PA. The light is at that certain slant that Emily Dickinson doesn't describe. It's the 'Fuck it. This is the only moment that ever was or ever will be' slant. It hits Annie full in the face. She really is illuminated. She doesn't blink. She looks me straight in the eye.

"I want you bad," she says.

We walk back to the house. We sit on the couch. It's still warm where our bodies had been a few minutes earlier. This time there's no space between us. Annie pulls my face to hers. She kisses me, full on the lips. I snuggle my face between her breasts. I love her skin, especially the V between her breasts. The skin there is more furrowed and wrinkled then the rest of her. Beyond the V on Annie's breast are the places where the sun doesn't shine, pale, tender. I like those places, too.

I trace my finger down the leathery skin of one breast and up the leathery skin of the other breast. I like the feel of her skin on my fingers. I can see through her blouse the dark mound of her nipple swelling up, a hard little seed that I want to swallow. Her bra pushes her breasts together. I put my hand between them. Warm. Soft.

"Ah," Annie says, and kisses the back of my neck. She slides her hands down my back into my jeans and kneads the muscle of my ass. She always does this. I always want her to do this.

Annie gets on top of me. I feel her full weight. Mouth to mouth, breast to breast, belly to belly. Her hips plant me farther into the couch. My hips reach up to her. She slides both hands under my ass, takes a firm hold of each cheek and pulls me even closer as she pushes down. We get a rhythm going, a dance. We move, her belly, my belly, her thighs, my thighs. I can feel the soft fleshy mound between her thighs and the hard bone beneath pushing into me, my own flesh and bone pushing back. We're touching everywhere, pressing every place we're able to press. The pressure and the movement gets more intense. Our tongues are in and out of each other's mouths. Our hands are grabbing, pressing, kneading any piece of flesh we can work except the one spot that wants pressing most. Our pants are down around our knees. I have one leg completely free. My legs are slightly parted beneath her. She could lift up and slide her hand between my legs. I could reach up and find her hot and wet, too.

She's working me. Everything in its time. I'm so wet. I'm so ready to get wetter. For god's sake girl, hit the spot. It's time. Come on, honey. I want it both ways, to be full, completely filled up, and at the same time completely empty, all the way open so it all spills out. Touch me, girl. I want to explode. I'm squirming under her.

The phone rings. Ignore it. Keep moving, keep moaning, keep your flesh heaving against mine, Annie. The phone rings again, unnatural intrusion, blasphemy of the rites of spring. Annie's mouth is on my breast now. She's biting my nipple. *A little harder, baby. Oh. Annie. That's exactly right.*

The answering machine clicks on. My voice, "Sorry we can't come to the phone right now..." The machine is on the end table, six inches from our heads. It's turned up full volume because my hearing's not what it used to be. I try to shut it off, but it falls to the floor. My girlfriend's voice comes blaring over the damned thing, "Hey, baby. You out in the garden? Plane's delayed. What a gorgeous day to be stuck in the airport. Hope you're enjoying it. Love you. Call you when I get to Pennsylvania." *Click*.

Annie makes a valiant effort to ignore the sound of the busy signal coming from the fallen receiver. She keeps on playing with my breast. But for me, there's a line where pleasurable erotic pressure becomes "stop right now" pain. It's the point where you hear your girlfriend's voice, talking sweet on the answering machine, while your ex-girlfriend has her teeth sunk into your right nipple.

I feel a stabbing ache from my nipple to my crotch. My body stiffens up like frozen roadkill. Annie tries to soothe me. She tongues my nipple softly, strokes the side of my face. I try to melt back into her, but I'm chilled to the bone. A shiver runs up my spine.

Annie sits up. She doesn't try to hide her annoyance. "Sandy sounds well," she says.

"Jesus," I say, "Jesus Christ Almighty."

"What's he got to do with it?" Annie asks.

"Sweet Mary," I say.

"Well, that's a little better."

I sit up next to Annie. "Sorry," I say weakly.

"I thought you and Sandy had an arrangement," Annie says, in exasperation, rearranging her magnificent breasts in her bra. She glares at the answering machine. "Progress," she says. She picks her blouse off the floor. I watch as her fleshy breasts slowly disappear under checked cotton, button by button. I stand on one leg trying to pull the other leg of my jeans and my panties up at the same time. I fall back onto the couch.

Annie stares at me. "Look at you. You're shaking. Poor baby." She puts her arm around me. She's more concerned than annoyed now. I put my head on her shoulder.

"Sandy hates the arrangement," I whine.

"Wasn't it Sandy who used to carry on about compulsory monogamy?"

"That was five years ago when she had the hots for her sister's neighbor. She's decided that open relationships work better in theory than in practice."

"All theory. No action," Annie sighs. "Never mind. I still love you, you sexy thing." Annie knows me well enough to know it's going to take me quite a bit of time to unthaw again.

I say, "Shit."

Annie stands up, pulls on her pants, tucks in her blouse. "I'm going home," she says, "to finish this business we started together all by myself."

She holds my face between her hands and gives me a suction-cup kiss on the forehead. That's what I like about Annie, she takes life as it comes. She's not angry, still a tad irritated, but what the hell, she's got the right.

"Thanks, Annie," I say. "I love you, too."

I watch her as she moves toward the door. I'm a lump of deflated libido. I see her through the window as she walks toward the daffodils. I watch her bend at the knees and lean forward. Her sturdy thighs support her. Her butt sticks out. This posture suits her. Her curves perfectly complement the landscape of the garden. Does she know that I'm watching her?

She sure does. Beautiful, mellow old girl. She's trying to direct my attention to the flowers, but I'm looking at her. Her smile is upside down. The garden is only a backdrop. Annie's the focal point. My spirit rises with her as she stands, waves at me and points to the flower she holds in her hand. Her grin gets closer and closer as she walks back toward the house. I turn the knob. It's warmer outside than it is inside. The warm air spills in my door. Annie offers me a daffodil, fully bloomed, from my own garden.

WINNER TAKE ALL

Andrea Dale

"Okay, contestants, listen up," the DJ said. "We start in five minutes, at eight a.m. sharp. Remember, one hand has to be on the vehicle at all times—your whole palm and fingers. You can switch hands as long as one is fully on the car. Except for during the fifteen-minute breaks, one every two hours, which I'll announce. You may not kneel, sit, lean, *blah blah blah*."

He didn't really say, "Blah blah blah." I just tuned him out. I knew the rules by heart. I'd been *prepping* for this contest.

Yeah, it's tacky and stupid, the whole "keep your hand on the car longer than anyone else and win it" schtick, but the fact was, this truck would be a godsend for the nonprofit I managed. Even if I didn't win, the publicity would help tremendously.

But I was here to win.

I stretched, bending over 'til my palms touched the ground (thank you, yoga classes), and continued to size up my opponents.

I'd placed myself between the two people I thought would be least competitive. One was a nebbishy-looking guy, on the thin side, who kept nervously pushing up his glasses. I was banking on him forgetting and pushing up his glasses with the hand that was supposed to be on the truck.

On my other side was a pretty, petite blonde. For the life of me, I couldn't imagine why she'd want or need a truck. She didn't look the type to set foot in one. She was wearing painted-on jeans—probably designer, but I wouldn't know designer jeans if they were cupping my own ass—and low-heeled gray boots. Her makeup was impeccable, her big blue eyes made wider by the judicious use of mascara and her luscious lips glossed a lick-able red. I suspected she didn't usually wear jeans; she looked like the type who wears little skirts and high heels.

Nothing wrong with that, if that was your thing. I certainly enjoy looking *at* pretty women in little skirts and high heels, and fantasizing about getting up under those little skirts and seeing what kind of panties—if any at all—they're wearing.

I'm not a skirt-wearing type of girl myself, and today was no exception. I'd dressed for comfort: jeans, sure, but broken-in, soft ones that wouldn't constrict movement; sneakers with gel insoles; and a T-shirt advertising my nonprofit.

"What's the Kensington Bird Sanctuary?" the blonde asked maybe ten minutes after we'd gotten started. She had a light, breathy voice, which suited her. Her dangly silver earrings caught in the light as she cocked her head at me.

"It's a rehab facility for birds of prey," I said. "I'm the manager. We could really use this truck to transport injured raptors to our facility."

Her laugh tinkled. "Oh, see, that's not fair," she protested with a little pout. "You're trying to get me to sympathize with you and lose."

I shook my head. "Not at all," I said, and it was true. She'd asked, after all. "I just automatically try to drum up support. It's the curse of running a nonprofit."

"All right, then." She favored me with a dazzling smile, even white teeth and juicy lips. "I'm Grace, by the way."

"Teddie," I said, waving my free hand.

"Nice to meet you," she said. "*Very* nice to meet you." Her voice went a little lower then, and I swear I saw her look me up and down and up again. She delicately bit her lip.

Was she flirting with me? Really? I couldn't imagine it, but it still gave me a little tingle. I cleared my throat. "Ditto."

She asked me a bit more about the sanctuary, and I learned she was a buyer for a chain of fashion boutiques. The more we talked, the more I realized for all her cuteness and little-girl voice, Grace was smart and accomplished.

After a while, though, I was feeling antsy, so I put my other hand flat on the truck, pulled off my first hand, and turned around. I made nice with the nebbish guy for a few minutes, but he wasn't all that into chatting.

The first contestant to call it quits did so after the first break. One down, eight to go, and the truck would be mine.

If I didn't get too distracted by Grace, that is.

Her shimmery gray top was cut low, so if she moved just the right way your eye was drawn to her cleavage. Well, my eye, certainly, and the eye of the guy on the other side of her.

Over that, she had on an open-knit shrug that tied just under her breasts, enhancing the view. The crimson matched her lipstick. Her outfit was simple, yet all pulled together—it really was an *outfit*, an ensemble, as opposed to some clothes she'd just thrown on that morning.

Me, I'd never gotten the hang of that. My idea of "layering" is throwing a hoodie on over my T-shirt when it gets chilly.

The guy on the other side of her started chatting her up. Big surprise.

She gently rebuffed him, her voice sweet, her smile brilliant.

He wasn't the type to take no for an answer.

"Look," she said finally. "You're not my type. *Really* not my type."

He made a final try.

"You want to win this thing?" Grace asked. "Then stop. Talking. To. Me. Because if you don't, I'm calling the ref over here to say you're harassing me, and who do you think he'll believe?"

The guy retreated, but I barely noticed. I'd heard something unexpected in her voice. A steeliness.

At first I thought I imagined it; it didn't fit with her breathy voice.

My rational brain may have insisted that I imagined it, but my body clearly heard it—and reacted to it.

Right down in my three-for-five-dollars cotton panties.

Grace turned and flashed me her dazzling smile. "It's all about psychology," she said. "The psychology of getting people to do what you want. It's about figuring out what *they* want. Putting your hand on a car for hours and hours, just to win it? It's like a psychological form of bondage. Being told, *Don't move*," and as she spoke her voice got that steely undertone again, the one that made my inner muscles clench.

I straightened my back, like a new recruit snapping to attention...or a submissive posing for her mistress.

I heard Grace's breathy chuckle, and I knew she knew what I was thinking.

"Oh, yes, just like that," she said. "Some folks like cuffs and ropes and shackles—need them, even—but others...others know *choice* is as good a restraint as anything. It's all about power, and most people think the top has power, but that's not true. The bottom does. The bottom *chooses* to submit. Holds her hands out for the cuffs. Presents her sweet ass for the spanking. Doesn't come until she's told to—or comes on command, anytime, anywhere."

My head reeled even as my nipples snapped to attention faster than my back had, and blood rushed to my groin, making me aware of my clit, my lips, the way my panties clung to my crotch.

That innocent, breathy voice coming out of that pretty little blonde form.

Aren't dommes supposed to be tall, imperious, stern and wear black leather? Not petite, angelic, smiling and wearing ruffly colorful fashion?

Maybe that's why she was affecting me the way she was. She wasn't a cliché, wasn't someone who used the tired old props.

In other words, she didn't need a dungeon to be a domme.

The DJ called another scheduled time-out.

Argh.

The showroom had only one tiny ladies' room, but Grace and I were the only two women left. She let me use the bathroom first, which was nice, except...damn.

Damn if I didn't want to plunge my hand down into my jeans, into my cotton panties, and stroke away the slick, needy urge she'd raised in me. A few minutes of privacy, that was all I needed.

But I knew she was waiting outside. I knew she'd know what I'd been doing.

And somehow, I didn't want to disappoint her. It was crazy, I knew, and yet I also knew that if I got myself off, I'd be... disobeying, maybe?

Grace hadn't said a word about what I could or couldn't do—and, indeed, we'd only just met, so who was she to give me orders anyway?—but I instinctively understood what she expected of me, and I wasn't about to let her down.

No matter how desperately I wanted to.

It was hard to pee, being this aroused, but somehow I managed. I staggered out of the restroom feeling flushed and desperately unfulfilled.

Grace gave me a stunning smile and a bottle of water then headed into the bathroom.

She also patted me, every so subtly, on the bottom as she sailed by. She didn't say a word, but I swear I heard "Good girl," in my head.

The local TV station came to interview us, asking each of us why she or he had entered the contest. The nebbish guy surprised me by saying he wanted to use it to pick up chicks. Of course I used the opportunity to talk about the Sanctuary; how we relied on donations, how important this would be for us.

I somehow managed to not sound distracted. I'm a good public speaker and I could talk about the Sanctuary for hours, but I also know how to distill it into a few pithy sound bites. Still, I could smell Grace's delicate perfume, and I was constantly aware of the throbbing wetness between my thighs.

Plus I was dying to hear her answer to the question.

She laughed, the sound a gentle and genuine delight. Even the camera guy instinctively smiled.

"Oh, goodness," she said. "I just can't resist a challenge, you know?"

Then, as soon as the camera swung away, she winked at me, and I got the distinct impression that winning the truck wasn't really the challenge.

I was.

I squeezed my legs together and immediately regretted the action, since it just made me hyper-aware of my sodden crotch, my aching clit, my empty pussy begging to be filled by beckoning fingers.

As the contest wore on, she continued talking, her light voice spewing filthier and filthier things pitched low enough for only me to hear. Of course, as the contest wore on, people dropped out, so the remaining contestants adjusted themselves with more space between each of us.

Except for Grace, who stayed close to me...and I, admittedly, made no attempt to move away from her.

Close behind me, she whispered, "What's your poison, Teddie? Restraint? Cuffs and ropes and shackles, even if they're not needed? Orgasm restriction or forced orgasms, over and over? Blindfolds and gags? Spanking, whipping, caning?"

Behind my eyes I envisioned everything she was saying. Grace coming toward me with silvery handcuffs and chains spilling from her small hands. Grace wearing a strap-on dildo, her slender hips rolling as she thrust into me. Grace standing over me, holding a paddle, raising her arm...

And, almost ridiculously, in all of the scenes, Grace's makeup was perfect. She would never, I knew, break a sweat. And her nail polish would match the leather of the harness she wore, burgundy or royal blue or purple.

My palm, where it lay against the truck, was slick with sweat—in fact, I could see my handprints all over, from all the times I'd switched hands. The small of my back was slick with sweat, too, and I knew I was flushed.

"Answer me, Teddie." Her voice was light and airy, laced with control and command.

"Yes," I blurted. "All of it. Whatever pleases you."

Without thinking, I started to turn, forgetting to put my other hand down before I started to lift my first hand.

"No!" Her hand shot out and pinned my wrist, keeping my palm flat on the side of the truck. It was the first time, in this whole long day, that she'd touched me flesh-to-flesh. The sudden feel of her fingers encircling my wrist, restraining me, triggered the long, slow roll of a mini-orgasm, coiling in my belly and uncoiling in my cunt in a series of shivery spasms.

My knees almost buckled, but I caught myself. Then I almost jumped out of my skin at a shrill whistle behind me.

"No touching the other contestants!" the judge, a florid-faced auto executive, barked. "Number Four, you're disqualified."

Grace was Number Four.

I remembered to change hands appropriately, even though they were shaking from the remains of my orgasm. "No, it's okay, she wasn't trying to distract me or anything, she's fine—" I protested.

"Sorry, those are the rules," he said.

I thought about calling him an ass, but that wouldn't have looked good for the Sanctuary, so I bit my tongue.

"It's okay," Grace said, with a dazzling, sweet smile that made the judge's shoulders untense, just a little. "He's right—I wasn't paying attention, and I broke the rules. She deserves the truck more than I do, anyway."

But before he could lead her away, she went on.

"Win this truck, Teddie," she said, in the same tone she might use if she were commanding, "Lick me until I come." She leaned in, ignoring the judge's frown. "If you do," she whispered, "I'll punish you. But if you don't…"

She shook her head, and then she was gone, leaving me with a whiff of her perfume and a final sharp tremor in my clit.

And I knew if I was the last person standing with a hand on the truck, I'd win a hell of a lot more than the contest.

LESSONS FOR LEONA

Tenille Brown

If her daddy had had his way, there would have been a party. Something big and nice to welcome her home from six years down South, but Leona had told him no.

She knew he meant well, but she also knew that she was too old for parties. Leona hadn't had one since her Sweet Sixteen and hadn't enjoyed one since she was twelve. Now she was grown, twenty-four in fact. She could drive and vote and smoke and drink liquor. And she had done all those things and more. She'd had five lovers and had even broken a heart or two.

But she couldn't really tell her daddy about that.

She couldn't really tell her daddy anything right now, as he sat across the table from her, scooping them generous servings from a salmon casserole.

"Tell me if you like it," he said, as he leaned back in his chair and folded his arms.

And Leona forked up a small bit off her plate and chewed, nodding.

"It's good, Daddy. Did you make it?"

She figured it might have been something he took up while she was away, like his pottery and the woodworking he had dabbled in after her mother died. After all, Leona had been dabbling in body painting and snapping nude photos of gorgeous women in her own spare time.

But her daddy responded, "I didn't make it. Ida did."

A new girlfriend? No. He would have said something.

Leona's eyebrows wrinkled in vague recognition. "Oh, yeah. That caterer," she said.

Her daddy nodded. "Right. I get her to bring the food in for our meetings."

Leona took another bite of the casserole and said, "Well, she did a great job."

And her father was as excited as if he *had* made it himself. Then he said, "She's agreed to give you a few pointers in the kitchen."

Leona swallowed her bite of casserole. "Agreed?"

"Well, yes. I saw her in town one day and I mentioned that you would be coming home soon and you weren't too familiar with the ways of a kitchen so she suggested—"

"*She* suggested?"

"Okay, I asked. Anyway, what's the harm? It wouldn't hurt you to make a potato salad and fry a few pieces of chicken now and then."

Leona dropped her fork and folded her arms. "Then this is about your ongoing love affair with deep-fried poultry?"

Her father half smiled. "What can I say? I like my fried chicken."

And that was okay, Leona supposed, since everyone had her weaknesses. Tall, golden women with nice, strong legs happened to be hers.

She realized her father was talking again.

"Surely you made friends with some of those girls down in Georgia, and not one of them baked a chicken in front of you or made a bowl of macaroni?"

Leona twisted her lips in thought. Yes, she *had* met Southern girls indeed, many Southern girls, and they had taught her many delicious things, but none of them involved a pot or a stove.

And none of them, not one of them cared that she couldn't cook, not Mindy or Sylvia, or even Bethany, but her father wouldn't want to hear that.

It would be nonsense in his eyes, some foolishness she learned at school, so Leona let it be.

Besides, he was so pleased with himself that it was almost cute and the hopefulness in his eyes and the twitch at the corner of his lips let Leona know that he was seeking the same excitement from her.

So, Leona smiled wide and took another bite of the creamy casserole.

Then she shook her head and said, "Just tell me when, Daddy."

Leona wasn't exactly sure what to wear to a cooking lesson, so she settled on a tank top and jeans. Ida, who lived in a small cottage on the outskirts of town, came to the door in shorts and a T-shirt.

Leona decided that shorts really suited Ida, the way her long legs extended from beneath them. In fact, Leona thought as she studied Ida's brown knees, she might mention to her that she should consider never wearing a pair of trousers again.

Leona had never noticed the rebellious kink of Ida's hair, the way it sprouted from her scalp in fuzzy curls that she had dyed strawberry blonde. And Ida's lips were full, pink without any lipstick, moist without any gloss. She wore a tiny diamond stud in her left nostril and two silver hoops in each ear.

Ida smelled like lilac. Leona assumed it was powder. And she might have asked, but she didn't know Ida that well, only that she was a few years older and minded her own business.

So, instead of saying all these things, Leona extended her hand and introduced herself.

"I'm Leona," she said. "My father tells me I could learn a thing or two from you."

Ida smiled. "I don't know if that's true, but I told him I would show you some of what I know."

She let Leona in.

Leona observed Ida's vibrant choice in furnishings, the orange wing-backed chairs, the golden loveseat. The wood of her coffee table and curio were dark. Her hardwood floors were clean and glossy.

Leona lingered behind Ida, her ears attentive to music playing softly in the background, something jazzy by a woman with a deep, raspy voice. They made it to Ida's roomy kitchen where she had various bowls and pans set out.

"I don't normally give classes, but your daddy was persistent, carrying on about the duties of a lady and whatnot. You planning on getting married or something?" Ida arched an eyebrow.

Leona laughed and shook her head.

Ida continued. "Well, at any rate, I figured I could keep it simple and show you meat and potatoes, fried chicken and gravy, but that would be a blatant waste of time and energy. I'd much rather show you those really special dishes for those special occasions, for romantic nights when you want to impress someone special. Like this."

Ida offered Leona a small bowl with dark, oval shaped fruit and thinly shaved nuts scattered about. The sweet smell of coconut rum wafted through her nostrils.

"They're figs," Ida said. "I let them soak in the fridge overnight. Take one."

Leona took the fig and bit into it. The juices from the fruit and the rum danced on her tongue, tickled her throat and warmed her chest. The almonds were crispy and were a nice effect to the sweetness of the figs and the rum.

"I'm going to use them for a fig rum loaf."

It was a simple lesson, in which Leona spent only an hour and a half in Ida's kitchen. Leona giggled when she left, because she was starving.

The loaf would need to sit for twenty-four hours before it could be eaten, Ida had told her, so Leona walked home, figuring that she'd have a turkey sandwich later.

And maybe it was the rum. Or maybe it was the jazz. But late that night after Leona had eaten her sandwich and she lay alone in her bed, she remembered the taste of rum and the smell of coconut, she remembered pretty brown legs and a head of curly, golden hair and she parted her legs and reached down and thinking of Ida, she pleasured herself until she grew tired.

Ida was a wonderful teacher. She'd been on this earth thirty-one years after all. She had seen things, tried things, and Leona felt like her little stint in Georgia was nothing in comparison.

Leona smelled the fresh herbs Ida waved back and forth in front of her nose. She had never even heard of thyme, couldn't quite tell the difference between cilantro and parsley, and Ida had decided that since Leona was still scorching rice after two weeks of lessons, maybe they should meet three times a week instead of two.

Not that it bothered Leona. She had grown comfortable

being in Ida's house, sitting at her table, standing in front of her stove, leaning on her counter.

And now, she was watching Ida set aside the herbs and squeeze a lime over a pan of shrimp.

"You have to be careful cooking with citrus," Ida said. "It tends to dry out your food. But the shrimp will cook fast anyway so we don't really have to worry about that."

But Leona was more interested in rubbing the lime across Ida's lips and licking the remnants off.

She realized that she was still admiring Ida's lips when Ida said, "You know, Leona, if you don't start paying attention, you won't be any better a cook than the day you walked in this kitchen."

Leona shrugged. She playfully pinched at Ida's waist and continued to ignore the comment. "Anyone ever tell you that you're remarkably thin for someone who cooks so well?"

Ida tucked her chin. "I suppose it's because I nibble."

"And you never stop moving."

And Leona never stopped watching her. She watched Ida walk from the stove to the island in the middle of her kitchen, from the table to the sink. Leona watched the perspiration roll down Ida's neck, watched her calves flex and release, watched the muscles in her thin arms contract as she lifted pans and casseroles.

"What about you? You work out to keep in such good shape?"

Leona sucked her teeth. "My father seems to think I'm getting bigger by the minute."

"And what do you think?"

"I think that I like to eat and everything I put in my mouth sits on my hips like a couple of saddlebags."

Leona couldn't be sure, but she thought that maybe Ida

glanced down at her hips for verification.

And it was then that Leona decided she should kiss Ida.

It was a simple kiss on the neck. Leona was certain it wouldn't hurt anything. And maybe Ida wouldn't even notice it. And if she didn't notice that, surely she wouldn't mind a tongue on her velvety collarbone or a hand on her elbow that slid down her arm and locked loosely around her wrist.

And as it turned out, Ida didn't mind any of these things. Ida sighed as if these very things were what she had been waiting for all along. So, Leona held her by the waist and brought her close. She kissed her on the lips. They shared the taste of lime on each other's tongues.

Leona knelt in front of Ida, brushing her cheek against the front of Ida's flowery dress. Leona lifted the dress, held it in a bunch at Ida's waist. She kissed each side of Ida's stomach and sucked gently on her navel.

And somehow, finally, they found their way down to Ida's kitchen floor.

Leona slowly lifted Ida's dress and pulled it over her head to expose her red panties.

Leona was wet at just the sight of her, at the thought that she was seducing Ida. And Ida, she was smiling.

Ida's back arched at the feel of Leona's tongue on her nipples. She giggled at the light sensation of Leona's breath on her lobe.

And when Leona smelled the hint of lime and could barely smell the shrimp anymore, the telltale sign that the meal was done, Ida came on her own kitchen floor.

Leona kissed Ida on her knees, ran her fingers across the softest parts of her thighs.

She whispered, "I'm hungry."

* * *

Leona was sitting in her father's kitchen thinking of Ida when he asked, "So, you learning much over there?"

And Leona smiled and said, "Yes, I'm learning lots."

In fact she had learned just recently that Ida was quite ticklish, that the tile on her kitchen floor had six different colors in it, that Ida's favorite color was blue, that her cottage had been handed down to her from her great-grandmother and most important of all, she learned that Ida loved strawberries.

Leona had fed them to her last night after they had rolled around naked in Ida's bed for nearly two hours. They had eaten strawberries and drank champagne and Leona had stayed the whole night.

Her father nodded, satisfied. "Good," he said. "You'll have to cook me something soon."

"Yes, Daddy," Leona said. "I will cook you something very soon."

Then he lightly pinched her arm.

"Looks like you might be doing a little more eating than you are cooking in my opinion, though."

And Leona had to keep herself from blushing. Ida had said that she liked the extra fluffiness on her. That it made her warm and juicy.

And warm was what Leona felt as she thought about seeing Ida in three hours. Juicy was the feeling between her legs as she thought of Ida coming to the door and greeting her naked.

Leona leaned back in her chair, stretched, and waited.

It was supposed to be almond-crusted tilapia, but Leona had let the thin pieces of fish bake too long and they stuck to the bottom of the pan because she hadn't used enough olive oil, so the only thing salvageable were the almonds.

Leona watched Ida place them on her lips and swipe them into her mouth with her tongue.

"I burned Daddy's ribs, too," Leona said.

Ida laughed. "I'm sure he didn't mind."

Leona shook her head. "No, he was pretty pissed. He loves barbeque. He told me in about three different ways that I had ruined a damned good slab of meat."

Ida chuckled. "You'll make it up to him. I'll fix you up a tray and you can pass them off as your own."

Leona shrugged. "Maybe. I don't know if it'll fly, though. I'm going to have to start explaining myself soon. All these lessons and the only thing I'm really learning to do is set off smoke detectors."

Ida came closer. "Surely that's not all you've learned to do, Leona."

And she reached for Leona's hand and placed it between her thighs. Ida lifted it up so that Leona's palm was resting against her cunt.

Leona felt she was warm there. And Leona, she was warm, too.

And soon, Leona was no longer worried about the fish. Soon, she lay with Ida in her bed kissing Ida's fingertips, shoulders and knees.

Ida tasted better than anything Leona had ever dreamed of putting into her mouth. Ida was bitter and sweet, she was tender and moist.

And when Ida came against Leona's mouth, Leona was full, full as if she had dined five times at the center of Ida's hips.

They often talked after, which was how Leona learned that Ida was a Gemini and grew up in Syracuse and was never formally trained to cook. It was also how Leona learned that in six weeks, Ida would be leaving for Paris.

Leona had reached up and smoothed out Ida's thick eyebrows. But now she brought her hand back down, quickly, as if she had been scorched.

Ida would be personally trained by French Chef Something-or-Other and as Ida went on and on about it, Leona looked at her, looked for some sign of remorse that she had to say the words, or even better, that suddenly she thought she might change her mind and stay after all.

But Ida just kept talking.

"A spot suddenly became available. And all this time I've been telling myself that it's just too late, that I'm too old for any more lessons and I already know everything I need to know, but it's a very coveted position. I'd be a fool to turn it down."

The excitement in Ida's voice made Leona smile in spite of herself.

So, she said, "I understand, honey. I would go for it if I were you, definitely."

Leona said the words only because she knew she had to say something. She said the words because, otherwise, she would cry. And Leona was twenty-four years old, and that was simply too fucking old to cry.

Ida was talking again. Her voice was soft and raspy now.

She turned to Leona and said, "How do you think your daddy would feel about it?"

Leona hoped Ida couldn't detect the change in her voice. She hoped that the tears wouldn't roll down her face and fall onto Ida's arm.

Leona said, "Well, I know he loves your fried chicken, but he'll find another caterer for his meetings."

Ida laughed. "Silly girl. I'm talking about you. I'm talking about you taking off with me. What would he think about that?"

Leona tucked her head in the crook of Ida's arm and inhaled the light scent of lilac from her skin.

No, Leona wasn't sure how her daddy would feel, but she was already imagining herself awakening with Ida in a foreign land, eating new and exciting foods that Ida would cook for her and feed her from her hands. Already Leona was imagining whispering words in broken French in Ida's ear.

As she chopped red potatoes, tossed in fresh scallions and added sour cream and mayonnaise, Leona agreed that maybe, yes, every young woman should learn how to cook. She herself had caught on, finally.

She stirred her pot of green beans. She covered the pound cake she had left cooling.

Her father would be happy with the meal, and he would most certainly be proud of her. And he would love the fried chicken.

He'd be just tickled about the whole thing.

And Paris. He'd get over that eventually and maybe one day he'd even be happy. Leona set up the dinner table nice and pretty with a six-pack of her daddy's favorite beer in a bucket of ice.

Leona wished she could be there to see the look on his face.

But instead she would be sitting in the passenger seat of Ida's convertible. And by the time he found the note, she and Ida would be on the plane.

And seven hours after that, Leona and her lover would be in Paris. They would both learn new things: Ida the ways of French cooking; Leona, new ways of loving Ida.

And that, Leona knew, was the most important lesson of all.

MORNING COMMUTE

Penny Gyokeres

Morning. Alarm, get out of bed, pee, feed fish, shave, shower, brush teeth, dress dyke-to-die-for in CK boxers, Carhartt and steel-toed breakers. Thirty-one minutes.

Coffee. Strong, large, homo milk splashed in. Get on the subway. Eight minutes.

Commute. Read digital paper: war, riots, famine, recession, murder, six-hundred-billion-dollar Apple, nuclear arms, hatred, violence, world's smallest lizard discovered in Madagascar; awesome. My stop: off the train. Nine minutes. Up the escalator while checking smart phone Next TTC: Bus in three. Walk off escalator and see you. Morning routine shattered.

Three minutes turn into thirty seconds as I pretend to flip through my smartphone with heavy-duty case, eyeing you all the way. New job? Interview? Not a regular. In six years on the same bus, I've never seen you. Black brogues gleaming with buffed polish, pant-cuffs ironed, pleats crisp, butt round. Black leather jacket perfect fit to slim waist and strong shoulders. Black, trim hair screams *dyke*. Nose and ear piercings catch sunlight sifting through grimy depot windows. You look up and see me, I glance directly at you, shades covering my eyes that take you in, outwardly full of nonchalance, inwardly captivated. No smile from you, no smile from me. Butch dance.

I move toward the platform and ensure I almost graze you, seated on the bench. Not looking back, I feel you rise and follow as I exit through the doors into the cool morning air. I turn on the platform; you are behind me, flipping madly through your smartphone with heavy-duty case. I stand still: you stand still next to me. We flip in silence, electricity flashing between us. The bus arrives. I sit; you sit across from me, able to see me in peripheral. I face you and cannot avert my eyes beneath my shades. We are still flipping as the bus departs. Four minutes.

If I knew you, we would be fucking. We would sleep in, late for work or appointments or interviews, and not caring. We would sleep in and be late because the night before we would have been out and up late.

You said pick you up at eight: dinner for two then a little dirty dancing, *per se*. We were dressed identically; black steel-toe garrisons polished, black leather jackets and chaps gleaming. Only subtle differences defined our one from the other. Your T-shirt said EAT ME, mine said BITE ME. The jeans covering your ass were black, mine blue. Your hair was black, short, curled with gel; mine light brown, shaved short.

We held hands into the restaurant, eyes locked: hungry. Ravenous actually. Eating was divine in your company and I know you felt the same way about mine. One hundred and six minutes.

Out of the restaurant, hands locked, straight to the not-so-straight kinky queer bar where we were welcomed with warm smiles, sly glances and lusty leers. Ice-cold beer in hand, you pulled me to you and whispered for my ear only:

Fuck me tonight? I squeezed your ass.

No, fuck me.

Play first?

No, just fuck me.

'K.

Planning an evening was that easy with you.

We were surrounded by sex; patrons dripping, shirtless; hot-as-hell staff; porn offering suggestions on the big-screen. My cunt became a throbbing brute. Beers flowed and I had to piss. Big shock...so did you. Bathroom was dimly lit and steel, stalls were dimmer and offered guaranteed good times; just dial...you hauled me in. Guaranteed good times.

Our lips met with fervor, supple butch lips wanting every taste of our kiss. Tongues intertwined, needing full submersion. Calloused hands grasping leather pulled us closer: tough, butch hands. My cunt was gripped, full-hand-hard through my jeans; I was so fucking wet. My earlier request was honored as you slid my hand over your open fly. Dick. Hard-rubber-no-questions-asked-dick. *Fuck me.*

Fingers first, I got a taste of and for your lust. Fuck and ring finger to open me up: index and pinkie heading toward my ass, palm pressed and powering my clit. My back leaned against the stall wall, steel and black leather hard against each other. My legs were open, my chaps and jeans well below my ass as you gave me a warm-up before the meet. You dipped down to run your tongue over my clit, depriving me of my kiss. I wasn't worried. *Fuck, don't stop!* Fingers in my cunt, mouth hard over my clit: I'm coming dyke, don't even bother with that cock, your hands and face are bliss! *Not so fast, butch.*

Your eyes rose to meet mine and I tasted my lust on your

lips. *Hmm, horny?* Said quiet while the guy pissed in the urinal behind steel only inches away. Fuck you. Really? Cocky now that you've got your cock in your hand and my full attention. *Fuck me, fuck I need you in me.* Your body hard and covered in leather like mine, working with me as I slid slightly down, legs spreading just enough for your blissful black brilliance. Fuck that feeling.

Your cock impaled me. My cunt was so amazingly ready. Lips held to yours, tongues tasting full mouth, I was stonewalled in ecstasy as you crushed my body to the steel behind me. No more minutes in the day. Nothing more than us fucking dykes. Your strength pumped and hauled my body back and my cunt forward. I grasped the leather of your shoulders as the wonder of your cock filled me and I came. My legs gripped your hips grinding: rhythm in tandem. Your tough hands grasped my ass and pulled yourself into me; I was in heaven for fucking you. I came again and again: lips locked to yours, releasing my passion through every pore in my body.

I loved the way you fucked me, every time, every way. Gasping together with me, you pulled out and grinned that cocky grin; you know I love it. Let's get home, the morning's only just begun. Two hundred and thirty-four minutes.

You ring the bell one stop before mine. Fourteen minutes.

I barely remember getting on the bus. I wonder if we're thinking in tandem, flicking and swiping away on our smartphones. My screen timed out ages ago, its blackness stares back at me, daring me to fill in the blanks. You stand, turn your back to me, head to the front of the bus. I look up at you full-on through my shades, willing you to look back. The driver opens the door and you step off, but not before glancing back at me, right back at me, and I know we are on the same page. The door closes behind you and I sit, grinning in my seat under the red of the streetlight. I stand and ask the driver to open the door again. I call out to your back, not twenty feet ahead of me: "Hey, can I buy you a coffee?"

You turn, and say, "I thought you'd never ask."

Fuck, I'm going to be late for work...

AFTERMATH

Valerie Alexander

It had been over a year since Kai left me, when I drove over to her new house. My visit wasn't intentional. She'd ordered takeout from the Thai café where I worked, but I didn't realize the address on the delivery slip was hers at first. The thick August heat had fogged my glasses, and when I took them off and squinted at the slip, the name GRUNDER at the top jumped out at me.

I started to shake.

Visions of everything she could possibly say to me filled my head. Apologies, explanations. I knew she was still living with the woman she'd left me for, Venetia Dale, because every dyke in town would have told me if they'd split up. I tried to imagine her opening the door and saying, "Come on in," Venetia waving from the kitchen like *Hey, it's been a year, let's let bygones be bygones*. Once I would have said Kai was too sensitive to do that, but that was before the night she told me it was over, and asked me seven minutes later to cry in the bathroom because I was upsetting Slater, her dog.

I turned the corner. I could have gone back to the café and made someone else deliver it, and I probably should have, but instead I pulled up to her new house. It was a big gray Victorian, shaded by towering elms. There seemed to be a large fenced-in yard, which complicated the mystery of why she had left Slater behind with me. I pulled up to the curb, adjusted my sunglasses and got out, bag in hand. There was a taste like cardboard in my mouth as I walked up the porch steps and knocked.

Venetia opened the door.

I had disliked Venetia Dale for years, before Kai even met her. Everyone in town knew of her; she was a performance artist and she performed everywhere she went, from long, melodramatic stories at the salon to holding court at cocktail parties to theatrical speeches at the gallery where she worked. She was a walking spectacle of artifice, from her white-blonde hair to her made-up name to her fluttery, actressy gestures. Practical Kai falling in love with her was an insane idea, I would have said once, but that was what happened and it upended everything I knew.

Venetia leaned against the door in a black polyester slip. Her platinum hair was in disarray around her shoulders and her mascara had flaked under her eyes. Her bare lips looked oddly flat and pale without their signature dark-red, creamy lipstick.

She looked like sluttiness crossed with heartbreak. It was the first time I'd ever seen what everyone found so beautiful in her.

"Hello." I held out the bag like I delivered food to her all the time. "That'll be fifteen eighty-three."

"Come in." Venetia swept out her hand like a conquered sovereign conceding defeat.

I'd never wanted to see their house. I didn't want to know where Kai ate breakfast or what new dog she had adopted when

Slater had watched out the window for weeks after she left. The shades were pulled, but I could see the house looked like an empty Pottery Barn set, exposed wood beams over cream walls and hardwood floors. I tried to picture Kai living here, her surfer girl muscles sprawled on the sofa and her ruffled leonine hair on the throw pillow, and couldn't.

A scratchy old Van Morrison album was playing. I remembered it well. Kai had an immense LP collection. "Nice house," I said.

Venetia's thin shoulders moved in a shrug as she moved the turntable needle to a different song. She slumped on the sofa. "You won," she said, and picked up a green glass. She swirled the liquid around before drinking.

"I what?"

"Come on, Becca. You were dying for Kai to leave me."

They were over. Now I knew why I was so calm in this house: Kai's absence. "I didn't even know," I said. "Not everything revolves around you, Venetia."

She gave me an *I deserve that* nod. Narcissists always know how to feign humility.

"So," I said. "That's fifteen eighty-three."

She looked up at me with tragic eyes. "Don't leave. Please? You're the only one who knows her like I did."

I started to bristle, but got control of myself. "I can't help you."

She finished her drink. "It's been two weeks. She didn't even take her records with her." She started to cry.

I was surprised at how little I cared about this. They had broken up, *so what*. Kai was still gone. It was only amazing that it had taken me this long to find out.

But I sat down on the other sofa and listened to the Van Morrison song fill the almost empty room. I could see into the kitchen from here, another magazine room of exposed brick and copper pans, and I tried to picture Kai having her daily breakfast burrito with Diet Coke in there. I couldn't. There wasn't even a ghost of her in this house. She was so gone.

"I went to a party last night—I have to leave the house at night or I go crazy—but all I want is her back. You're the only person I can think of to talk to. And now..." She gave me a crafty look. "Here you are."

I couldn't help it: I smiled. I thought of everything I had lived through this last year and what now awaited her.

"Amazing that this happened," I said. "Who would have thought *Kai* would be the type to just walk out on someone."

She wiped her nose. "I know you think I'm an asshole—"

"I've thought that for a long time."

"But I am not a home-wrecker—"

"You are totally the type who loves to think of herself as a home-wrecker. Femme fatale, Venetia Dale."

"You don't even know me, Becca."

"Just stop. Even right now, you're making it about you. You don't know how not to be the center of attention. Who cares what I think of you?"

But I was talking too much and showing that I did care about this situation. I got up and walked into the dining room and looked out the varnished oak French doors. The backyard was slightly overgrown, a deathly afternoon stillness hanging over the grass. A half-grown black Lab puppy was watching the doors with his chin on his paws, and he got up, tail wagging, when he saw me. A woman with short hair, finally come back to him.

I walked back into the living room. She swallowed and made a visible effort to be composed.

"You're not what I expected," she said. "I thought you'd be more femme."

I ignored the implication that she hadn't known what I looked like. She had known where to order her lunch from, after all. Instead I pushed the bag of takeout at her and said, "I'm sorry you're so upset. You should eat something. But I have to get back to work, Venetia."

"You could come back later," she persisted. "And talk to me."

"Except I don't want to."

Her eyes narrowed in speculation. I had just lied and she knew it. I felt oddly riveted to this house that was a mirror world to my own, one year ago. Some pang of nostalgia recognized the fresh grief and bewilderment hanging in the rooms. This was my house when I was only weeks past coming naked in Kai's arms. When her socks were still in the bureau, her conditioner in the shower, signs that she hadn't really left for good. Nights when I refused to change the sheets so I could still smell her in them, humping the bed facedown as I fingered myself and buried my face in her pillow.

I looked at Venetia in her black slip and smeared mascara. She was foreign to my world. Yet she was also Kai's most recent sexual landscape, the last recipient of her mouth and body. It was Venetia's sheets that smelled like Kai now. I wondered if Kai liked to come on Venetia's tits the way she liked to come on mine.

Venetia got up and moved the needle again to the start of the album. "Tell me what's going to happen," she said. "You obviously know her better than I do."

"If she left her records behind, I don't know her at all anymore."

I walked into the kitchen, despite a vague awareness that it was rude to wander the house like it was my own. And there it was under a surfboard magnet on the fridge: a picture of them toasting the camera with shot glasses, Kai sunburned and grinning. It was true. Their relationship had really happened. I looked at another picture, more formal, of Venetia in a vintage dress and pouting at the camera like an Old Hollywood star. Unbidden images of their first date flooded my mind. How it must have felt for Kai to fuck a woman so different from me, so skinny and feminine and artificial and demanding. Prom queens and actresses had never been my taste or hers and I wondered exactly what she found down that rabbit hole that was so enticing it lured her away from her entire life.

I walked back into the living room. "Sorry," I said. "I do have to get back to work. Eat something, you'll feel better."

Venetia leaned back against the sofa cushions, swirled her drink around and finished it. Then she glanced up at me, calculating.

I knew I had to leave right then and failed. Instead we looked at each other for a long moment. Then she straightened and pulled her slip over her head, throwing it on the hardwood floor. She leaned back again and opened her legs.

A fierce and carnal curiosity roared through me. How revolting: I was attracted to Venetia Dale. I couldn't stand her and yet it was like a piece of Kai watching me from the sofa. Venetia was my amalgamation of loss and sex and answers made flesh.

My heart gave an odd thump. "Okay."

She didn't take her eyes from me as I moved toward the sofa. I looked at everything that had been Kai's: long legs, small pointy breasts, a bit of slack to her stomach. Venetia had such a long, hipless body, not at all like mine. Her skin was so pale against the dark blue sofa that she didn't look real. She didn't look like anyone I had ever slept with.

I unzipped my shorts and took off my tank top with the desultory detachment of changing at the gym. But my heart was pounding. Venetia avidly examined my every detail for what I knew were the same reasons I'd stared at her. Leaning forward, she ran her fingers down my leg, squeezing my knee slightly. She took my hips in her hands and looked up at me. "I can picture you two together," she said.

"We were together for almost five years," I said. My clit was so hard it hurt. I took her chin in my fingers. "No performance."

She gave me a clever look one moment before her tongue lashed over my clit. Her small hands fluttered between my upper thighs in a *spread* gesture, then got to work, lifting up the hood of my clit and parting my pussy lips. She was opening me up and consuming me like I was a piece of cake long coveted, efficient and hungry. My fingers curled in that white-blonde hair as her agile tongue worked me over. Three fingers were moving inside me, then four; then her entire hand was inside my cunt, filling me up with shockingly dominant pressure. This was the same head Kai had gotten for the last year, Venetia's small hand in her pussy and her tongue on her clit. I was the interloper in a ghostly threeway they probably never intended to have. But Venetia's dark-blue eyes met mine and I knew that Kai was the ghost here.

Something long frozen in me was thawing and breaking up, relief and warmth flooding my body. I pushed Venetia back against the sofa and knelt over her, brazenly humping her face. I'd fucked four women since Kai left me but this was the first time it felt real, an acute awareness of her small breasts and soft hot mouth filling my senses. We weren't going to be done here until I'd mapped and devoured every inch of her, fucked her every way possible. Raw lust suffused my nerves, a tumult of grief and sex building into an insistent tension, and as Venetia sucked my clit, I came in six brutal waves that I rode out shamelessly on her mouth.

I leaned over the couch, breathing hard. My body felt so incredibly light and hot, as if I had restructured the laws of time and space.

Venetia caressed my damp hair. "I knew you wouldn't play games."

I was exhausted and exhilarated. I pushed Venetia on her back. She spread her long legs wider than I'd ever seen any woman spread, offering up her pussy as if it was the holy grail that had lured Kai away from me. I pulled at her longish pink lips and rubbed her tiny clit, thinking of all the other women we'd slept with before Kai and all the women waiting in our future. Nothing meant anything but what was happening right now.

I slid three fingers inside her. Her cunt closed around me, tight and quivering. She groaned but I took my time, absorbing her warmth and her smell. I stroked her clit and her front inner wall in tandem, slowly, making her kick the cushions in frustration. Then without giving her time to adjust, I fucked her hard and rapid until she was bucking and panting beneath me. Venetia gripped the sofa cushions, groaning out unintelligible sounds and writhing until her small tits bounced in time with my hand. I'd always assumed she would fuck like a pillow princess but she was exploding under me, all wetness and heat.

I withdrew and slapped her thigh. "Get on all fours."

She obeyed, unexpectedly elegant as she looked at me over her shoulder with those mascara-smeared eyes. I ran my hands up her lean thighs and then took command of her pussy and ass, fucking both in a seesaw rhythm. She dropped her head and howled. How I wished that I was packing, but then again, watching her cunt close around my fingers was spellbinding. Liberation flooded my mind and it mixed with the smells and cries filling my senses until I felt electric with power.

Venetia rocked her skinny hips back to engulf my hands and then she groaned as her pussy squeezed around me, a rhythmic release that ended when she collapsed onto the sofa in a cloud-burst of tears.

I stroked her back. The album had played out to the end, the needle repeating its rhythmic coda: bump and scratch, bump and scratch. Venetia crawled into my lap and hooked her arms around my neck and we began again.

I HAVE A THING FOR BUTCHES

Sonya Herzog

So I have a thing for old butches. Sue me.

Okay, not old. Older. Somewhere around sixty. A *real* butch.

You know the type I'm talking about. They're a dying breed. The youngest ones are about fifty, and the oldest...well, they'll be hard butch as long as they live. Not stone. No, I don't mean the true transmen who didn't have all the modern options for change. I mean the real butches. Chivalry and men's clothing. Short spiky hair usually peppered with gray. As often as not, they're wearing women's underwear, whatever kind their mothers made them wear.

And that's how they are: all hard and masculine on the outside; all soft and 100 percent woman on the inside. They have names like Laurie and Julianne and Caroline, and they're either too old to have bothered changing their names to tough things like AJ and Sam and Drake, or somewhere in that middle period where they took on hippie names like Bear and Blue Jay and Sunny.

I love everything about older butches. I love how they'll open a door for me and then stare at my ass as I walk through. But yet, when I try to catch them at it, they're looking me in the eye every time. I love how they'll get up to do anything physical for me, even when I'm younger and could do it just as well. I love how they each have their own area of expertise that proves they're a successful part of a man's world, whether it be motorcycles or line cooking or accounting or something with animals. I love how they'll squash a spider one minute and the next will scream like a little girl over a snake. I love how they move, with a masculine assurance and swagger, and a woman's gentle tread. And I love how they feel: strong arms and hands, and maybe a little softness around the middle. I love how they can do all the things a man can do, all while making me feel like the center of their universe. And I love how when things get hard, they're woman enough to lean on someone rather than pretend they can do it all alone.

You get my point already, yes? I love a real butch. And I love to make love to a real butch.

I go to this womyn's gathering every year. Twice a year, actually. It's a small writer's retreat where we all get to know each other a little bit at a time over the years. A few new womyn come each time, but there are plenty of us who've been coming for years and always will if we can.

Every six months I go to this retreat and drool over the butches. There's Laurie, who looks so much like a man you sometimes have to do a double take, until she opens her mouth and has the voice of a small woman. There's Bear; she can cook a meal and serve it up with a smile; she's small and dresses like a '50s greaser. There's Sunny, whose eyes make me want to melt; she comes with her high femme partner and they sell icies out of an old ice-cream truck.

I love to sit on the rock wall outside the dining hall, pretending to write, and watch them go about their business. I love to flirt with them across the salad bar. I love to accidentally bump into them. Feel their hands steady me, and look into their eyes while they offer an apology, even though they're not at fault. I love to tease them about not going swimming on the hottest days, when all us femmes and soft butches are already in the water.

I've been enjoying these retreats for a bunch of years when this year something changes. There are no cliques at this retreat. Lunchtime comes and we all sit willy-nilly together. And this time, Laurie sits down right across from me. It's the first time I've really talked to her. We talk about what we write, where we live, what we do to pay the bills. I ask her opinion about a piece I might read during the evening open mike session. She likes it. We both go to turn the page at the same time, and her hand brushes mine.

I'm already on fire. It's been too long since I was with a woman. I see a blush rise to her cheeks and think maybe it's mutual. I offer to share a few other pieces; it's an opening of myself with no risk to her. She bites, so we find a quiet corner with some uncomfortable chairs (because there are no comfortable chairs at the retreat).

I watch her read, her eyes moving over the words, her expression subtly changing with the poetry. I'm not fool enough to hope for more, I'm just enjoying this little bit of Laurie that's all mine.

She smiles when she finishes. Sits for a moment. We talk about the pieces, when I wrote them and for whom, if they're still true. She says she'd like to get to know me better. Can she take me out to dinner? I bite back my urge to yell, "Hurray!" and offer a demure, as-femme-as-I-can-make-it, "Yes."

She takes me out to dinner. Casual place, good conversation, lots of eye contact. She comments on how I hold my knife and fork, European-style, never putting down the knife. She takes my hand. I can feel her pulse. Or maybe it's mine, which is hammering in my throat.

Back at the retreat, she gives me a hug. At first I think it's too chaste, but then I realize she's put her whole body up against mine. As I wrap my arms around her, I can feel her back muscles bunching with her movement. I can feel her breasts pressed against my own.

I want more, but I'm no fool; I know how I should play: real butches call the shots. Femmes make themselves available. They bat their eyelashes, they accidentally brush their hands along exposed skin, they stick out their breasts and wiggle their asses. If they're really brazen, they wink. They do all this to let the butch know they're interested, but the butch has to do the asking. The butch has to take on the risk, so if anyone's at fault, it's her.

I'm not a traditional femme. I play by my own rules, leaving the butch enough control to feel safe, while taking enough to make me feel empowered. I push my whole body against hers, trying to melt into all the spaces between us. I squeeze her hand as we part. I turn back to look her straight in the eye and thank her for a wonderful, if too-short, evening. I smile. I don't wink.

The next evening, I do my open mike bit with Laurie in the audience. Volunteers serve a late-night snack after, and she brushes against me as she moves past to the end of the line. Then she's sitting with some of her friends, and I'm doing the same. But our eyes keep meeting across the room. She looks down first once, then I do. She's definitely pursuing, and I'm not fleeing.

It's late. I hug my friends and walk into the evening coolness. The retreat has a number of small, bare-bones, hotel-style cabins and a dining hall. The walk between the buildings at night is refreshing, with large starlit expanses between the cabins and only a few porch lights. It starts out that way tonight, and then all the sudden I'm warm. Hot, actually.

Laurie calls my name. I turn to watch her saunter up to me. I want to reach out and touch her, but I leave that to her. I turn toward my cabin and she falls into step with me.

"Can I walk you to your room?" Her woman's voice is strong. She's not really asking a question so much as presenting me an opportunity to stop things before they go too far.

"I'd like that." I want things to go too far.

When we get to my room, I stand aside for her to come in. I lock the door so there's no chance of interruption. Perhaps this is going a bit too far, but maybe she's trying to understand a femme of my age. I'm nearly twenty years her junior.

She smiles. "I was going to do that."

In an instant, I'm shy. I'm blushing, and I don't usually blush. But I have nothing to fear. She's a real butch and knows how to handle the situation.

"Can I hold you?" Still standing, she opens her arms to me.

I take the three steps across the room to her, and she folds me in her arms. My head is tilted up, and her lips come down to meet mine. She's not much taller than I am, just enough to make me feel the physical differences between us. Her kiss reminds me of the similarities. Her lips are the soft fullness of a real woman. Her feet are planted wide, and her strong arms hold me, which is good, because I might fall over otherwise.

The kiss is electric. It's hot and wet and tongues and lips. My hand is on her face and I feel her jaw working with the kiss. There is nothing else. There is only this kiss.

She pulls back, ever so slightly, and breathes, "Wow!" before plunging in for more.

We kiss for hours. No, I know that's not true. We kiss for what feels like hours, simply feeling each other responding in kind. After an eternity that I do not want to end, I feel her reach for the hem of my shirt and lift it. I move to make it easier, letting the shirt slip over my head, and watching her slowly release it to fall on the floor. The cool air from the open window touches my skin and makes my nipples pucker. I wasn't sure she could see that in the dim glow coming in from the porch light, but she reaches out a hand to brush one of them, and I shiver.

Then I am shy again. I like to be clean for sex. I like my lover to be clean too. I try to put on my best demure femme face and ask, "Shower?"

She nods. Takes my hand and pulls me into the bathroom. The showers are short. There's only a stall, so we don't even try to share it. She comes out of her shower after I'm already dried and primped enough to satisfy my femme ideals.

Even in the almost nonexistent light, I can see her dark nipple pointing toward me through the steam. It's too tempting. I bend down, looking at her until the last possible moment, and run my tongue over her nipple. She lets out a little breath, and puts her hand behind my head. I lick again and again hear her sigh. And then I wrap my mouth around her nipple and start to suck. Gently at first. You never know how hard or soft a woman likes it. I suck harder as her hand tightens on the back of my neck. She moans.

She releases me and steps back.

I give her room to dry off and do what she wants with my toiletries. I'm trying not to rush things. Let her set the pace. When she looks at me again, I back out of the bathroom until the backs of my knees meet the bed, which isn't very far.

She comes to me and we mold our bodies together in another kiss. Only this time there's no clothing between us. The shock of her skin on mine makes me glad I've got the bed for support. The electricity of the kiss ratchets up a notch. I only know this isn't a dream because no dream feels this good.

Then it's Laurie's turn to look shy. "I don't have anything with me..." she mumbles.

I don't know what to say that won't overwhelm her, so I turn, reach down, and pull my toy bag from under the bed. I always travel with my toys—you never know when you might need them, if only for a solo act.

She looks at the bag, then steps around me and sets it on the bed. A small smile touches her face when she pulls out the dildo and the vibrator. Then she breaks out into a big grin when she pulls out my fully adjustable leather harness. I rub my breast against her arm as I put the lube on the bedside table, just in case.

Laurie wastes no time or effort in putting on the harness and securing the dildo. Then she looks at me and pauses, as if I'm supposed to do something. I revert to what I know best: I take her other nipple in my mouth.

She likes a lot of sucking pressure, and I love the feel of her nipple in my mouth. Her breasts are surprisingly firm. When I reach over to play with the other nipple, she deftly turns the tables.

She pivots us around until my back is to the bed again, and applies enough pressure to let me know I need to be on the bed. Now. My heart is pounding in my chest and I'm already wet. As I slide back on the bed, all the way up to the pillows, she slowly crawls after me.

I thought she might go slowly, take her time, try teasing me for hours. But it's not her style, at least tonight. She spreads my legs and lowers her tongue to my other lips.

Oooooh. The first touch of a warm wet tongue on my clit.

There's nothing like it. She knows what she's doing. In a matter of minutes, I'm writhing on the bed.

"Please…please…" I beg her to change position.

And she does. She kneels between my legs, her body upright, and enters me with the dildo ever so slowly. I could take a plunge. But the way she teases me brings my hips rising up to meet every slightly longer thrust and makes me pant with desire.

There are various murmurings and moanings as she fucks me. She knows what she's doing. She's rough enough to make me want more and gentle enough to make me want more. I want more.

When I finally moan I'm going to cum, she lets herself go. She lies down on me and thrusts the full length of the dildo. She kisses me again, deep and hard and needy. I feel the moan rise in her as my own orgasm peaks. And, as I'm coming down the other side, she lets out a deep-throated groan signaling her own orgasm.

She starts to pull out of me, but I hold her still. She raises her head just enough to look at me with a lovely smile on her handsome face. Her hair is spiked out in every direction, and it's very sexy. She kisses my eyes and my cheeks and, gently, my mouth.

There is still electricity.

When I'm ready, it takes only the smallest movement to start her withdrawal. She unbelts the harness, lays it on the bed and comes to stretch out next to me.

I wake up freezing from the open window a short time later. Laurie is breathing softly next to me, and the sight of her warms me. I can't resist running my hand over her body. Featherlight, I let my hand wander across the hills and valleys of her skin.

Tanned hands and arms give way to pale breasts with dark nipples. Her stomach is soft, but flatter than I thought it might be. Her pubic hair is in tight, still-damp curls. I hear her breathing change as my hand explores, and then it catches as I touch those curls.

When I get a positive reaction, I do more. So I tickle the curls. Run my hand along the crease where thigh meets mons. I leave the area to run my palm over the curve of her hip before returning to repeat the movements.

She rolls, or rather lets herself relax, onto her back and spreads her legs ever so slightly. I repeat my gentle exploration, then run only the barest tip of my finger along the cleft between her lips. She moans. I watch her as I do it all over again. Her eyes are closed, her lips parted, her hands completely relaxed.

She spreads her legs wider and bends her knees, giving me open access. Somehow I know if I dive in, she will retreat. So I tickle, and lightly run my fingertips over sensitive skin. With each repetition, I part her lips a tiny bit farther until finally, I bare her clit. I stick my finger in my mouth and then barely touch the tip of that wet finger to her already glistening clit. She pushes her head back into the pillows, arches her hips up toward my finger and lets out the most satisfying moan. And so I continue, with every touch as soft as the first. My fingers explore every moist fold. And when they are just at her opening, she thrusts her hips up to take them into her.

My body lurches with desire. I want to fuck her. She is so wide open. So wanting. So ready.

Maybe she *does* want it. Maybe, being a real butch, she can't ask for it. Won't ask for it. But maybe, just maybe, she wants it as much as I want to give it.

I continue with my fingers for a minute, taking them out to play with her clit, putting two fingers inside her. She is so wet.

"Stay. Wait. Trust me." I implore her as I quickly move away from her, retrieve the dildo and harness, and strap myself in.

She has to hear what I'm doing, yet she stays just as she is, eyes closed, hands relaxed, hips gently rocking. I mean to mount her, but the sight of her wetness makes my mouth water, and I have to taste her. She is sweet and salty and positively dripping. She keeps thrusting her hips up for something that's not yet there. So I kneel between her legs and place the head of the dildo on her clit.

I want to tease her. I want to make sure she's ready and willing. And she is. She moves her hips in such a way that I have no choice but to enter her. She wraps her legs around me and makes it clear, although she never says a word, that she wants to be fucked. Properly. Forcefully. Now.

I never thought I would have the honor of fucking a butch. I've had my fantasies. This is so much better. After I am inside her, she opens her eyes and looks directly at me. I know she wants it. I know she's all here with me.

I fuck her. And she takes it beautifully. Her legs wrapped around my hips, her hands reaching up to pinch one of my nipples, her hips rising to meet my every thrust.

Through all the thrusting and moaning and sweating, I keep a tight rein on myself. I could cum any minute. Only when her hands clutch the sheets, and she says "Yes," just once, do I allow myself to cum in time with her orgasm.

There's something about having an orgasm while fucking your lover. It's like there's a tunnel from my cunt straight through the middle of me, and the orgasm fills that whole inside space. The sensation takes over for a moment. It feels like forever, but it's only a fraction of a second.

When I return to myself, Laurie is letting out the last little moan from her orgasm.

As soon as she stops rocking, I withdraw, unhook the harness and let it drop to the floor, and then lie back down on top of her.

I want to protect her from whatever misgivings she might have. But she's fine.

She smiles up at me, kisses me, and then moves me to lie next to her. "I didn't know you could do that. Did you cum?"

I nod. "Was it okay that I...?" I let the sentence die out.

She nods. "More than okay. You're quite talented."

I smile.

We fall asleep until sometime in the early morning when the sky first turns gray. I wake to find her sitting on the edge of the bed. I can tell she wants to go back to her room, and I tell her that's okay. We both know this encounter isn't going to lead to anything more permanent. Well, except for perhaps a repeat performance in six months.

Did I tell you I have a thing for butches?

LA CAÍDA

Anna Meadows

When I was seven years old, I caught a monarch butterfly off the fruit trees in my grandmother's backyard. It had perched on a pear blossom, its wire tongue probing the center for nectar, and I trapped it in one of the blue mason jars Abuelita had once used to can cactus-flower jam. I watched it flutter against the aqua glass, its wings a flash of marigolds and obsidian.

"Let it go, *m'ija*," my grandmother said, pausing from her work in the herb patch.

"Why?" I asked.

"It's hungry."

"But so am I."

Worry crossed her face. Even after years of watching her granddaughters turn eighteen, when a hunger for salt and iron filled their mouths, she didn't know why I would want to eat the winged creature. My older sisters and cousins craved blood, only blood. *Naguales* never wanted anything else.

"Let it go, *m'ija*," she said again.

"Why?"

"He could be a warrior," she said, reminding me of the legend that said fallen Aztec soldiers were reborn as monarchs. "He could be your ancestor." She picked a handful of marjoram leaves. "And even if he's not, he could be *un ángel caído*."

"A what?" I asked. I knew as little Spanish as my mother; she'd forgotten all but the Lord's Prayer since her family moved to Luna Anaranjada when she was five.

"A fallen one," my grandmother said. "Sometimes God takes pity on them, depending on what they've done. An angel who rebels against Him will see no mercy. He'll be thrown to the Earth and vanish before he hits the ground." She pointed up toward the Milky Way, coming into focus and banding the sky as it darkened. "*Como un meteoro.*" She took the jar in her hands. "But for the lesser sins, he might turn the angel into a monarch on its way down, so it can float to Earth. Its wings turn to limbs only when they touch the ground." She eased the jar back between my palms. "Do you see, *m'ija?*"

I nodded, my eyes down, and unscrewed the lid. The monarch hesitated, crawling along the inside lip, but I shook the jar and it fluttered out.

I didn't hunger for another butterfly until after my eighteenth birthday, when I wanted blood so badly I was ready to bite into my own arm. My sisters waited out their cravings as my family had for generations, eating raw, bloody meat from a cousin's shop, biding their time until they heard about a man who raped a woman or beat his wife. They would surround him in one of the fallow wheat fields outside town and share the meal like guests at a wedding feast. When a village was rid of such men, we moved on.

They always invited me. I rarely came. The man's screams and the sound of my sisters' teeth tearing into his muscle turned my stomach.

Carmen made fun of me. "Little sister is hungry, but can't eat. She doesn't want to work for it. She wants to buy it in cartons at the store like orange juice."

I didn't hold it against her. She often led my sisters to their next meal, and because of our family, the talk about our kind, *los naguales*, was changing. Villages used to fear *naguales*. They called us witches, and whispered that at night we turned to cats and wild dogs to commit our crimes. They said we were why children became sick and crops withered. They blamed murders and missing livestock on our taste for blood.

Thanks to my family's penchant for the blood of men so evil no one missed them, wives and mothers now spoke of us as guardians. Good men used us as warnings to their sons and brothers. If they guessed who we were, they did not tell, fearing we would flee before we had rid their village of the kind of men we fed on. If one of those men found us out, he never lived to expose us.

No one ever found the bodies. My mother and Carmen never told me how they managed that. Once I asked them if it was the graveyards; two of my uncles ran a funeral home the next county over, and a few of my cousins worked as undertakers. But my mother only looked horrified and told me they'd never defile good men's tombs with the bodies of the depraved.

Depraved or not, I couldn't feed on them. My sisters had grown tall and lean on their diet. I'd gained ten pounds trying to fill the gnawing in my stomach with the olive oil cookies and *chiles en nogada* that were once my favorites. My breasts had bloomed a full cup size. My thighs had softened and widened, and I carried a little pouch of extra fat below my belly button that strangers mistook for baby fat, thinking I was still thirteen. I ate, and ate because I couldn't stomach what I needed. It wasn't that I objected to what my sisters were doing, to what my family had done for a hundred years. But my body rebelled against the nourishment. Carmen, for all her mocking, had brought me a glass of it once. But I heard the cries of the guilty man and their teeth puncturing his ligaments as surely as if I'd been in that fallow field, and I couldn't keep it down. I was eating myself into the next dress size, and I was still starving.

It shouldn't have surprised me that the next time I saw a monarch butterfly floating past a *pitaya* flower, I imagined its powdered wings on my tongue.

It was the night Hector Salazar stormed onto our front lawn, stinking of cheap mezcal and crushing the *datura* under his boots, and waking the whole neighborhood. "Get out here, *putas*! You filthy, murdering whores! You killed my brother!"

Carmen strolled onto the front porch, our grandmother's pearl-handled pistol tucked into her skirt. "Your brother tried to rape another man's wife." She cleared flakes of dried oregano from under her fingers, and tossed her head at Adriana, Lucia, and me to tell us to stay back. "God brings swift justice sometimes. It's not our place to question His ways."

He spat on our statue of *la virgen*. "I'll kill all of you." He waggled an unsteady finger at Carmen. "The sheriff thinks you're pretty. That's the only reason you're not in the jail. But it doesn't matter. I'll kill all of you myself." He stumbled over the brick planter border.

Lucia, pure soul as she is, stepped forward to keep him from falling, but Adriana held her back, and Hector fell into the weeds.

"Not tonight. I'll let you *putas* wait and wonder when I'll get you." He staggered to his feet, his knees and elbows coated in mud, and out toward the main road.

Adriana fumed. I gripped the porch railing so I didn't

tremble. When Lucia caught her breath, she cleaned *la virgen* with her skirt.

"Don't worry," said Carmen. "He knows what his brother did, and he knows he has nothing to threaten us with. Go to bed."

Carmen slept like a cat in sunlight, and Adriana and Lucia turned over in their beds until they wore themselves out.

I knew I wouldn't sleep until dawn, so I took a walk in the desert behind our house. That was when I saw the butterfly.

It looked already dead as it was falling. It flapped its wings no more than the wind would have done for it, and it tumbled toward the ground without riding the updraft. I lost sight of it and found it again, its path swirling through the dust that clouded the air.

I knew my grandmother couldn't see me. She'd settled with my mother in Cachcaba, thirty-seven miles away; we brought them blood in blown-glass jars on the weekends. But I searched the dark anyway, just in case. No one would ever know. If it was already dead, it couldn't be one of my Aztec ancestors, so what could be the harm? Birds ate butterflies every day.

A last gust of wind swept it up before its body weighted down its wings and pulled it to the Earth. I tried to follow it, but it vanished in the dull gold of blowing dust.

When the thin dirt settled, the butterfly was gone. In its place, a human body lay curled on its side.

I gasped. I didn't know how I'd missed it or how long it had been there. It looked dead, at first. From the cropped hair and straight hips, I thought it was a boy. Then I noticed the slight curve of her breast. She was naked except for bruising that darkened her back.

She was breathing.

I knelt behind her. I reached out to see if she was really there.

My fingers barely grazed the fine, peach-fuzz hairs on her back, but her shoulder blades pinched, her eyes snapping open. She struggled for breath like I'd just pulled her out of water.

"Shh." I stroked her back.

"Leave me alone," she said, her voice young, but low.

"You're hurt," I whispered.

"I'm all right."

"You need help."

She shivered, though the day's heat had barely faded with the dark; she must have had a fever. "Please leave me alone."

"I won't hurt you," I said. "I'll take you to the doctor. He's not far."

"No," she said. "Please. Don't let anyone see me like this."

I took my shawl from my shoulders.

It was light, just enough to guard against the chill that settled over the desert at night, but I draped it over her waist, using some of the slack to cover her breasts.

I caught another glimpse of the bruising on her back. It wasn't indigo or violet, shadowed in yellow. It was veined in black, and filled in with orange. Two great, bruised wings, like a monarch's, but out of focus, spread across her back.

I wanted to touch them. I didn't.

"Are you a warrior?" I asked, even though I doubted it; her hair was gold as new corn silk, and the tan of her skin looked dirty, not coppery like the raw sienna that ran in my family.

"No," she said.

"Are you one of them?" I asked. "*Un ángel caído?*"

She winced. It was as close to a nod as I'd get.

I took her in my arms. She was light, lighter than she should have been even with how thin she was, but she grew heavier as I came closer to our back door, like she was becoming solid and human. She fell in and out of waking, asking me over and over again to leave her alone, leave her out there. But when I put her in my bed and wrapped her in my grandmother's *ojo* blanket, she slept.

I needed clothes. She might let me touch her if I gave her clothes. The shops in town wouldn't open until morning, and the skirts Carmen, Lucia, and I wore would look strange on the *ángel's* boyish body, with her short, messy hair. Adriana's dresser was my only choice.

She was the heaviest sleeper of all of us. I eased her door open and snuck toward the heavy dresser. But my foot hit the only board in her room that creaked, and she started awake.

"Little sister?" She sat up in bed, groggy. "What are you doing?"

"Could I borrow some of your clothes?"

"Why would you want to borrow clothes from me? You never wear pants. Besides, they wouldn't fit you."

"Please?" I said. "I'll explain in the morning."

"Is there a man in your room?"

"Of course not."

She got out of bed, pushed past me, and slipped toward my room.

I followed after her, but I had to slow as I passed the hallway mirror and the side table I always ran into if I wasn't careful; my hip hitting its corner would wake my sisters for sure, especially if one of the earthen jars fell to the tile and shattered.

Adriana threw my door open and saw the black and orange bruising on the *ángel's* back. "You brought home *una caída*?"

I shut the door behind us. "She needed help."

"Carmen will have a fit when she finds out. She doesn't even like me going around with women. If she finds out you have one in your bed…"

"Then don't tell her."

She clicked her tongue all the way down the hallway and came back with trousers and a collared shirt. "These might be a little big and too long." She left them on the dresser and nodded toward the *ángel*. "She's cute. I can see why you like her."

"Adriana!"

"Don't worry, little sister." She eased the door shut as she left. "She's not the kind I like."

I dressed the *ángel* in Adriana's trousers while she slept. The shirt I'd let her put on herself. When she woke just after midnight, I heated a *chile relleno* in the oven and tried to get her to eat.

"I'm not hungry," she said, still a little asleep.

I looked over her bony frame. "You look hungry."

"So do you," she said.

"I'm not," I said.

"You still look hungry." She turned over, sucking air in through her teeth at the sudden pain.

"What is it?" I asked.

"Nothing."

"You're hurt. I knew it." I pulled the quilt from her shoulders, freezing when I saw the scrape on her shoulder, the one that had been against the ground. It glistened like liquid garnet, warm and alive, the blood of a living woman, not a dead man.

I caught myself biting my lip.

Even in the dim room, I saw the flicker of understanding in *la caída*'s face. "You're a salt girl," she said.

"What?"

"We call you salt girls, because you want the salt in the blood."

I swallowed to keep from crying. I wanted her warmth, and to run my tongue over that slick of blood so badly it was driving me to sobs. "I don't know why. We've been this way for a hundred years. Maybe more."

"Even we're not told why things are the way they are." She lowered her gaze, like shame was weighing it down. "Why we want what we want."

I pulled a strip of cloth over her wound, both to help it heal and so I wouldn't see it. I wanted to dampen the smell of iron, sweet as rain-made rust. "Why did you fall?" I asked.

A wry laugh stuck in the back of her throat. "Why do you think?"

"You wanted something."

"Yes."

"What?"

Two shallow breaths wavered in the back of her throat, one, then the other, before she grabbed me and kissed me, her desert-warm mouth searing my lips.

"Soft." She buried her nose in my hair and dug the heels of her hands into my back. "You're so soft." Then she dropped her hands and pulled away. "I'm sorry."

I stopped myself from grabbing her back. "I don't understand." I straightened my posture. "You fell because you wanted someone?"

"No." She dropped her head, letting her hair shadow her face. "That's the worst part. There was no one. I didn't fall in love. I just wanted."

I crawled on top of her, slowly pinning her down, and kissed her. She startled, but then gave her mouth to mine. I let my mouth wander down her neck toward her breasts, but it strayed, and her blood stained my lower lip. She arched her back to press her body into mine, but her blood heated my mouth, like hot sugar on its way to caramel, and I scrambled off her so quickly I fell from the bed. She grabbed my waist and pulled me back.

I licked my lip, blushing and guilty.

"You are hungry," she said.

"I shouldn't be," I said. "I eat all the time. My sister says if I don't stop, I'll get so chubby, I'll look like a little girl forever."

She pushed a piece of hair out of my face. "You don't look like a little girl."

I watched her mouth, her lips parted.

She turned her shoulder toward me. "And you're hungry for this, aren't you?"

I looked away. I didn't want to see the jeweled red again.

She cupped my face in her hands. "Could you live off me?"

I raised my eyes to hers. "What?"

"Could you live off me?"

I tried to wrench away from her. "I couldn't do that."

"Because it's not possible?"

"Because I couldn't do that to you."

"Yes, you could," she said. "I'm no good for anything else."

"You'd be weak whenever I had some of you."

"I don't care."

I snuck a look at the streak of garnet on her shoulder. "Would you let me give you something?"

She narrowed her eyes. "What?"

"What you wanted."

"I couldn't ask you for that," she said. "I'm fallen. I'm dirty."

I slid my hands under the sheet and onto her hands. "And I'm a *nagual*."

She moved my hands back on top of the blanket. "If I could be your nourishment, maybe I'd be something good again."

I got up from the bed.

"Where are you going?" She asked, baring the red jasper of her shoulder.

"I need a cookie." I paced in front of the door. "Do you want a cookie?"

"No. I don't want a cookie."

I put a hand on the doorknob. "Well, I need a cookie."

"Why?"

Because I still thought the food of my former life would fill me. "Because when I get upset, I want cookies."

She laughed a soft laugh. That made me madder, and I left.

I hadn't even closed my bedroom door behind me when the barrel of my grandmother's pearl-handled pistol was in my face.

"Good," said Salazar, his drunken breath pressing me against the wall. "The littlest *puta*. Come on." He gestured with the gun, and I followed the gleam of the handle toward the living room.

Carmen always kept my grandmother's pistol in the armoire in her room. I didn't understand how Salazar could have it until I saw my sisters lined up against the mantel, Carmen with a gash across her right temple. Their bedroom doors were open, and they were in their nightclothes.

"All four *putas*." Salazar shoved me toward them.

"Leave her alone," said Lucia, in a louder voice than anyone but her sisters had ever heard her use.

Salazar pointed the gun toward her. "The Virgin Lucia has something to say?" He twirled the barrel through her curls.

Adriana lunged at him, but Salazar jammed the hilt of the gun into the side of her head, and she reeled back toward the mantel.

Lucia stayed silent, glaring at him.

"Any of you whores have anything to say?" he asked.

Blood from Carmen's wound glistened on her eyelashes, heating her stare. Adriana held the side of her head, but glowered through the hair in her face.

"That's what I thought." He lowered the gun, but held it tight. "I want to hear what you did to him. I want to hear where you hid my brother's body."

La caída's face appeared in the hallway mirror out of the darkness, the steps of her bare feet quiet on the floor. She lifted a terra-cotta vase from the side table.

Salazar turned at the slight sound of dried clay against wood, but *la caída* had already lifted the vase over her head, and brought it down on Salazar's.

The gun went off, shattering the mirror in the hallway. Lucia screamed. Salazar fell to the floor, hitting his head on the ceramic tile.

I searched the dark for *la caída*'s face. She was nowhere.

I stepped over the glass shards. "*Caída?*"

I heard her soft moan and followed the sound. She was on the floor, her wound spattered with blood. I knelt to look at her. I hadn't remembered the wound as that big, that open.

It was on the wrong shoulder.

"He shot her," I said, feeling her forehead and brushing her hair out of her face. "He shot her."

Lucia grabbed her shawl. "I'll go wake Marcus."

"She's going for the doctor," I whispered to *la caída*.

"No," said *la caída*. "Please."

Adriana turned on every light in the hallway. "Get her away from the glass."

Lucia cleared a path with the broom and I pulled *la caída* away from the broken mirror.

La caída tilted her head, sweat dotting her forehead with glass beads. "Take what you need."

"No." I kissed her forehead. "No."

Carmen found the bloody bullet among the glass shards. "It's not in her." She held it up. "It grazed her." She crouched near us, taking in the black and orange wings on *la caída*'s back with a slow nod.

Adriana began boiling water on the stove. Lucia crossed

herself and whispered a prayer I couldn't make out.

Carmen held *la caída*'s arm by her elbow, not rough, but no more gentle than she had to be. "It's not deep. But you should see the doctor anyway."

"What will he do to me?"

"Nothing I don't tell him to," she said. "He's my brother." She looked at me. "Where did you find her?"

"Outside," I said.

She set her elbow back down and nodded at Lucia. "Marcus will come here."

"Aren't they going to come take me?" *La caída* asked, pulling her limbs into her chest.

"Who?"

"I killed him," said *la caída*.

"No one will know." Carmen tossed her hands toward Salazar's body. "Who's hungry?"

I couldn't lift *la caída*'s body anymore. She was heavy as a real woman. Adriana helped me get her back into my bed, where our brother checked her wound, pressing his lips together and nodding at my bandaging. "Not bad, *hermanita*." He gave *la caída* something for the pain, and she slept. "She saved all my sisters, huh?" he asked when he saw the lines of her monarch's wings. "Should be enough to get her back into heaven when she dies."

"What, now you're a priest?" said Carmen, shooing him out of the room when he was done. "Get back to your wife."

As my sisters took their meal in the fields outside town, I lay in bed next to *la caída*, tracing my finger along the thin cut where a shard of glass had sliced along the edge of her hip. Marcus had missed it because he was worried about the wound on her arm.

La caída moaned awake.

I pulled my hand away.

"No," she said, almost humming. "It feels good." She reached up, her eyes still half-closed, and rubbed a lock of my hair between her fingers like it was silk ribbon. "You're still hungry." She pulled the sheet back to expose the cut on her hip.

I flushed. "I can't. You're hurt."

"Will you take care of me?" She gave me a lopsided smile in the dark.

"Yes." I curled her hand into a loose fist and kissed her thumb. "Yes."

"Then take what I want to give you." She pressed her palm into her hip to thicken the little thread of blood. "Take what you need." She cradled the back of my neck in her hand and gently guided my mouth toward the cut.

Part of me wanted to drain her; I'd silenced my hunger for the months since my eighteenth birthday. But she was so warm, all salt and no sweetness, that I wanted to savor her like the wine of black Tempranillo grapes or the darkest bittersweet chocolate. I drank slowly, and before she was too weak I stopped and slid my mouth across her thigh to the triangle of soft hair between her legs. I sucked on her labia, one at a time. I touched her as I kissed her, and she shuddered when I felt her wetness, and again when my curious fingers made her wetter. I drank her wetness and tasted the same perfect salt I found in her blood. She pulled me on top of her and traced her hands under my dress. Her palms painted my shape so I no longer felt young and hungry, rounded with baby fat. Her hands and her salt were shaping me into something nourished and womanly. Soft.

Her fingers found me, and she touched me in the way I'd tried to touch myself every night for years. She covered my mouth with hers to keep me from waking my sisters. We mapped each other's bodies with our mouths, and when her touch made me as weak as she was, we slept.

When *la caída* was well enough, she and I joined my sisters on their walks, Carmen and Lucia with the lovers that followed them from town to town, Adriana with her woman of the week. As we passed the town cemetery, a headstone caught my eye. It was too new, too free of weeds and dry lichen, and carved with only the letter S and the current year. The grass covering the grave looked new and tenuous.

La caída stopped with me, but couldn't tell what I was looking at. She hadn't passed the cemetery a hundred times.

"Mother told you we would never defile good men's graves," Carmen whispered as she passed. "Instead, we make new ones."

La caída watched Carmen, and her eyes narrowed as she listened. She didn't yet understand the ways our family, how the undertakers and stonecutters, the doctors and butchers, all worked together to shield the desires of the women. She didn't yet understand how we worked, humans or *naguales*. She didn't yet know the million little sins we committed to turn our hunger for salt into the best thing it could be.

Carmen took my hand and *la caída*'s and put mine in hers. "Welcome to Earth, *ángel caída*. You have a lot to learn."

THE HORSE AND HOUNDS

Rachel Charman

They come from miles to be here, I think as I feel the car's tires scrunch on the gravel drive. Peering through the rain-washed windscreen I remember what you told me. You sat in my kitchen, a ray of sunlight on your hair and mouth, being an island of fun in this silent, open, empty place. You smirked at me, knowing you were twisting my heart with every filthy word as you told me when and where to show up. I hadn't known if you were teasing me or not. Now I am here, jittery at the thought of finding it all true, and I want to phone you in your new home with him and tell you that I have gone after all, to see if it hurts you.

The place is the usual English country pub, too far out from anywhere for a former city-dweller like me to walk to. It is square, brick and thatch, with a chipped wooden sign swinging and squeaking over the door: THE HORSE AND HOUNDS. It could be any pub anywhere in the country, but you—my lovely, teasing, unobtainable you—told me this place was special.

"They're coming from all over the county to this place, for

a little, you know..." you said, looking at me from the corner of your cat's eyes. I do know. I had seen that look on your face before, as your head rested on my pillow. It was a look that denoted pleasure; private, individual pleasure. Holding a coffee cup as you lay in my bed, one eye on the clock, because you knew your husband would be home for dinner within the hour, you told me about what happened that time at the pub, and that it was going to happen again. A week or so later you were gone, and I suddenly understood why you had told me to go there: to ease the pain of your departure.

When I walk into the place, holding a newspaper over my head to catch the rain, I am hit by two things: the hot, dog-like smell of pubs now that smoking is banned, and secondly, how inconspicuous the women are. I scold myself for my silliness. Had I expected them to be sitting beneath a banner? You would have laughed at that, in your high, sighing, skipping laugh that made your throat work beautifully.

I make my way to the bar, flapping my wet paper and tugging my coat open. I order a bitter shandy from the barmaid, who is a squarish, middle-aged woman dripping in bangles and earrings, and survey the women for a moment.

At a table in the farthest corner, partially hidden in a nook in the wall, is a group of six women. The age difference between them all strikes me, as I savor the first glug of warm, earthy beer. There is a woman headed straight for sixty if she is a day, but another who can't be older than twenty-two. I mentally shake myself again for making assumptions. Did I expect them to all look just like me?

In a way, though, they do all look like me. I can see, as I walk past the fireplace across the red, sticky carpet, the brand of loneliness in their faces. It's the kind of loneliness that hangs from the features of a woman's face, like moss or cobwebs; the kind of loneliness that builds up over time in this desolate place the rain never leaves alone. It is the kind of loneliness a chat at the post office, or the hand of a husband, or the glow of the TV can't wipe away; the loneliness of a woman with love all around her but who can't love, and who feels her heart is beating loudly and alone in all these wide open spaces; not thrumming in time with the world or someone else. My face looks like theirs now, since you left my heartbeat to slow alone.

I get to the table and the woman who is in charge, Justine, looks up and smiles. We had a stilted conversation on the phone a day or two ago to confirm times. She is around forty, with dark hair, and a fashionable wax jacket on her thin frame. I can tell from her accent and the slightly patronizing way she looks at her little group that she is a former urbanite like me, and wealthy to boot.

We exchange hellos. I hadn't really thought about what to say next but fortunately someone is pulling a chair over and someone else is shuffling along to make space and there, I'm seated among them with the least fuss possible. They don't want to draw attention to themselves. I feel as though I've just sat down with a new book group.

The conversation too feels like that of a book group. It is the nervous, extra-polite talk of women keen to make a good impression. I take them all in. Justine used to be something flash in the city before she and her husband upped sticks to the country to start a family. It is clear from her manner she is used to exercising authority. Kim, the young one, is plump and mousey with a baby at home with her farm-laborer husband. She's a local girl who has barely left the county. There is Marge, a weather-beaten woman in her late fifties, whose partner, who died last year, is alluded to regularly in non-gender-specific terms. There are two

thirtysomething friends, Sam and Lisa, with identical glossy hair-
cuts and trendy Ugg boots. It is painfully obvious, to me at least,
that they are lovers and think it is a secret. Then there is a wiry,
clear-skinned woman of indeterminate age, dressed boyishly in
denim and a checked shirt, her blonde hair cropped close to her
head and her hands writhing for want of a cigarette.

Into this I throw my story. Yes, I'm new to the next village,
having moved in just a year ago. No, nobody back at the cottage
I bought petulantly, believing I was too old to need city distrac-
tions anymore. What do I do? Well, I'm a writer. I don't mention
how I have barely written a word since I saw you over the
garden fence, tucking a strand of hair from the corner of your
apple-red mouth behind your ear. I leave out how I had hated
the place instantly but stayed because after living next door for
six weeks, you appeared in my kitchen and then in my bed, and
then came over every day at 12:00 to drink coffee and make love
while your husband worked without thinking of you. I forget to
mention that when he took the new job you refused to make any
plans to see me again, as if plans lent some sort of calculation
to our affair, whereas slipping in my back door every day you
seemed to be able to write off as a series of one-off slips of judgment. Then off you went, leaving flowers on the kitchen table as
the removal van belched and shuddered away.

He'd been trying to make you pregnant and you didn't want
him to. You said the feel of my skin on yours made you feel
like a woman and not a reproductive machine made of fluids
and membranes. Then you left me in this countryside hell, and
I ache.

Keeping all this to myself I observe for a while. The conversation steers toward neutral topics like the weather, the TV, and
the last good fair of the summer. It is not stimulating but my guts
are fluttering with nervous excitement. You had told me about

this little gang, and now that I can't have you I want to live in the little story you left behind.

You can't quite remember how it happened last time, you said, leaning on one elbow in bed, your hair soft and straggled by my hands. You whispered, running a finger from my chin to my breastbone, it actually was a book group to start with. Justine brought together this group of strangers and you went along for something to do. Perhaps it was because they were all lonely at the right time, or perhaps it was because the right amount of chardonnay was drunk. Several factors led to an occurrence, you said. Things were done, privately, you said. They hardly mentioned it afterward, you smirked as you kissed me, but then months later Justine sent out an email to say the "book group" was meeting again. "You should try it," you had said, and looked sad, although I didn't know why at the time.

I had turned up just half an hour before last orders, wanting to minimize any awkward chitchat. At 11:00 p.m., the bell rings and Maureen, the barmaid, starts slinging the locals out with a clanging singsong of "Finish up folks please!" As she trundles by with a cloth and a bottle of anti-bac spray, Maureen drops a key discreetly onto the table in front of Justine. Nobody else in the pub would have seen her do it, but we hear the light clack of the key on the wood and the mood steps up a gear. I sense them grow more tense. Justine, used to being followed, downs the vodka and orange she has been nursing and everyone else copies. Jen, the boyish blonde, tucks a roll-up cigarette behind her ear in preparation. As the last punter leaves and Maureen locks up the doors behind him, she nods to us. Justine zips up her wax coat and smiles at us, but her smile has changed. It's not the wide-mouthed, cheery grin of earlier, but a small, sly, knowing curl of the lips. Wordlessly we all get up and follow her to the side door and out into the passage between the pub and its surrounding walls. As the others file by I borrow a light from Jen. We exhale and I say, "What's in it for Maureen?"

"Last time she joined us," says Jen in a low voice as she walks ahead. "Not tonight though."

I want to say something conversational but Jen's tone tells me the time for jabber has passed and all my questions will be answered some other way. I smoke hard in the cold night air and follow her into the dark.

The six of us slip through the long grass at the back of the pub to the woods behind. Here the lights from the pub kitchen fade and I have to keep my eyes on Jen's coat to stay on the path between the trees. The air is cold and the leaves drip with rain that chills my hands and the back of my neck. I begin to feel jumpy in the shadows, feeling the mud slick under my boots. *This is how people end up chopped into pieces in the trunk of someone's car,* I think. Then Jen glances over her shoulder to check that I am still there. I like the strong curve of her chin and the sharp cut of the hair at the nape of her neck. I feel a flutter of vague, basic lust and follow.

We walk until we reach a large shed with brown paint peeling from its brick walls. Justine, with a sly glance up the mud path, unlocks the door and opens up. From my place at the back of the crowd I can smell the inside: earth, dead leaves, paint and wood. We file in.

Inside the place is dark until Justine lights a camping gas lamp and a few candles that stand on a chipped old coffee table. Moth-eaten rugs and a few damp cushions are scattered around the small, low space. We sit cross-legged on the floor.

The atmosphere presses down hard on all of us. There is an overriding sense of longing in the room, as if our collective wants are spilling out onto each other. Most of all there is expectation, a hint of desire, and something almost cannibalistic. I realize all eyes are on me. Kim and Marge are looking politely from lowered eyes, but Sam and Lisa are restraining the urge to nudge each other and nod at me. Jen is looking at me with the kind of bold, butch appraisal I would usually object to, but doing so would seem churlish under these circumstances.

Justine smiles levelly at me and places a hand on my arm. She seems to be the one most comfortable with what we all know is about to happen.

"I know a friend told you to come along," she says. "Did she tell you what happened last time?" She squeezes my shoulder lingeringly.

You did tell me. "I ended up sitting in the middle of them and taking everything off," you said. "I showed them how I do it when I'm alone," you breathed, your hand following your thoughts and my hand following yours.

I begin to unbutton my coat and Justine nods encouragingly. I pause after that, not sure if and how to go on. Jen, who had been leaning back in the shadows, kneels closer to me and removes my shoes, so tenderly and with such confidence that I realize whatever girl she is brooding over must have been worshipped.

I take off my shirt and jeans. I find it hard to meet anyone's eye as I do it, though I can see Marge's arm curled almost supportively around Kim's shoulders, while Sam and Lisa hold hands. I imagine you undressing here in the cold, under these women's eyes, and thrill to echo you as if it brings you closer to me.

I can feel the pent-up lust my still-young body naturally creates, but also, the deep-seated, instinctive fear of other women's eyes on my body, and most of all, the overwhelming pointlessness everything has had since you disappeared. I have halted.

This time it is Marge who snaps me out of it. She waits until I look up and meets my eye. She is steely gray and blue-eyed, with a strong, trustworthy face. When she speaks her voice has a rich timbre and a warm West Country burr.

"It's only flesh and blood, chickadee," she says. "Don't have to give us no more than that."

Somehow she sounds warm and wanting at once. I want to show her, this old and grieving woman, my body, my poor starved skin, and see how my pain might match up to hers. The thought of sharing something that is so close to passion—grief—turns me on and I slip out of my underwear quickly before I can change my mind.

I am naked in a darkened room with six women. I blame you for this. You always make me do things I wouldn't otherwise. I realize that I have been living every second for a year as though you have been watching me, even those hours when we were apart, and it has made me brighter. I have written not a word of the novel I set out to but the hundreds of love letters I have written to you, sent or not, are the best work I've ever managed. I couldn't have done it without you having drawn me clearer like an artist tidying up her masterpiece.

Jen is looking at me like a woman in a drought confronted with a lake. She is slim, strong, silent and sewn up with chivalry. I can see the lean muscle of her shoulders and the frown quiet, moody women wear. You taught me how to want a woman when I hadn't before. It is easy to want her, so I do. I decide to perform for her.

I place my hand on my neck, running my fingers from there to my collarbone, and sigh as the familiar lines of my palm graze my breast. I wonder if this is too quick or too coy for the group. I look at Justine, who has slipped off her coat and unbuttoned her Levi's. She is lying back on a cushion, still smiling around at us all as she trails her hand lazily across her navel.

I run both hands now to my hips. You loved to hold my hips.

The day we first made love, you came into my kitchen as was habit, and as I stood with my back to you making coffee you said I had the proportions of a model, but scaled up. I laughed hard, unsure of whether it was an unwitting put-down or an innocent compliment. Then your hands were on my hips and your breath on my neck and my world fell apart.

My hips fit into my palms as softly as horse chestnuts fit into their silky shells and for a moment I am lost in myself. When my hand sweeps to my thigh and then to the softest skin where my legs meet I hear a sigh—I am not sure whose—and I am aware of the women again.

I look up and see them in flashes. Justine is ahead of me, her slim hand working smoothly inside her jeans. Sam and Lisa are kissing tentatively, as though it has never happened before, nipping at each other's lips like nervous little birds. Kim has moved so Marge can cradle her across her lap, holding her in a close bear hug. Jen is still and soundless, her arms wrapped around her knees and her head cocked to one side as she watches me. I make it my mission to crack her. The need to make her react spurs me on as my fingers feather out across my cunt and I tip back my head.

In my mind's eye you are here. You watch me, as you watched me a hundred times in bed, as the thick bulb of my middle finger finds my clit; the thin, vibrant seam of me; and then the deep opening below, before moving away, teasing and tasting. I become aware of the curling smirk on my mouth, the one I didn't know I had until you pointed it out. Jen laughs in the back of her throat. She has seen that smirk before on the face of someone she loves. I settle into the smooth rhythm of my fingertips and open my eyes to see her crawling toward me on the grainy floor.

As she reaches me I see the others around beginning to let go as if they are in a sort of trance. Sam and Lisa, whose passion is so clearly near the surface, are the most susceptible. Sam has pulled Lisa's scarf and blouse from her and is planting thousands of hungry kisses on her shoulders and throat. They only have eyes for each other and are only here because they need this secret mania to truly show themselves to each other.

Marge has her hands—wonderful, leathery brown hands that held the same woman for years—gently planted around Kim's flushed round face. Kim is looking up at Marge with a kind of disbelieving joy. Kim slips up her own skirt and lavishes the attention her husband doesn't know how to give to her own full, curved legs. Justine has shrugged off her shirt and jeans and is touching herself at an unabashed, luxurious pace.

Jen reaches me on all fours, poised and curious. I wonder if she wants me to stop what I am doing to myself and turn to her. Although I'm not *au fait* with the roles we are all playing, I realize from her catlike position at my side that she is rarely, if ever, "done." It is clear from the way her eyes rush from my hand to my curling toes to the flush creeping up my throat that she revels in giving pleasure. She is waiting for permission.

I nod and she reaches out. She traces a cold fingertip across my starved lips. I haven't been kissed in what seems like an age and my mouth trembles at her touch. She lowers her head to the curve of my breast and begins a slow, expert journey across my skin with her lips and tongue. I gasp, thinking first only of the sensation, then of her, then of you. Her lips close on my nipple and her tongue makes slow circles around it, sucking harder as she shifts to lie beside me. I reach instinctively to stroke the smooth hair at the back of her neck and press her harder to me. She groans softly and is answered by a little half laugh from Justine. I see her watching Jen intently and realize she is the one Jen is pining for.

Around the room, the mood is thicker and watching them I feel my own desire harden. Sam and Lisa are locked together on the floor, their arms and legs entwined, kissing frantically as their hips grind together with increasing urgency. Marge is still cradling Kim, but now she is working her hand inside the younger woman in time to Kim's soft panting. Kim watches Jen and me, transfixed. I shut my eyes and listen to them all, the sounds of hands on skin and lips on lips in an ancient rhythm, almost trying to pick out those special sounds you made for me alone.

Jen climbs above me. Her mouth is on mine, insistent yet soft. She tastes of beer and tobacco and I smell her: hair wax, wet grass and cheap soap. I feel as though I am being unfaithful to us, then I picture you with him and I wrap my legs around Jen's waist.

Her belt is cold against my thighs and she is breathing hard against my neck. I tug at the buttons of her shirt and reach underneath. I press her breast hard, knowing she won't like to be caressed. She allows herself to arch her back and groan. She isn't like you. She is tough and moody and feels heavy. You were like sunlight in my arms. I want her to fuck me, to envelop me with brutal sensation and drive you away. I wrap both arms around her neck and press myself, hot and wet, against her jeans. She presses back and I growl, "Fuck me," into her ear.

The words increase the tension in the room. Kim, her former shyness gone, has raised her knees and spread her legs wide as Marge presses her whole hand roughly against her cunt. Sam is lying on her back, her hands over her own mouth, as Lisa kneels between her legs, licking and gripping Sam's hips. Justine is on her knees, her hand working furiously, watching us intently.

Jen's fingers push into me and I forget everything for a few seconds. She holds still within me, letting me tense around her hand, before she begins to push back and forth. She uses the power in her hips and back to drive her hand harder, her whole body working in a fluid wave. She has her eyes closed and mouth open in an expression of pure oblivion. I wonder if she is picturing someone else underneath her and it turns me on. I picture you fucking me like this and my body responds with another wave of arousal although my heart cringes. I kiss Jen, my mouth open, pushing my tongue roughly against hers. I squeeze my legs tight around her and grind my clit against her belt buckle. I am pushing savagely against her, forcing her to fuck me harder with her hand trapped between us, and she loves the aggression.

In a corner somewhere I hear someone come. With my eyes squeezed shut I can't tell who it is, but I hear the rushing thrust of hips and hands reaching a peak, then slowing and intensifying, then dying away. Like magic it works on the rest of us. Justine begins to make a low, humming sound in the back of her throat and Kim lets out a series of surprised, delighted gasps. The forbidden sound of another woman's most private pleasure adds to my own and I begin to feel the familiar tension in my legs and stomach.

As I build to my orgasm, coherent, reasoned thoughts are pushed aside and random images break free in my mind. I see hands and mouths and breasts and shoulder blades moving to my rhythm in my head. I see myself in snatches. I wonder if any of these women fucked you like this and the idea takes hold. In my mind's eye the women are in this room just as they are in reality but underneath Jen, bucking and gasping, is you, not me. I watch you in my mind, a drop of sweat clinging to the hair that falls over your eyes, your head thrown back, your toes crossed in that way that you do when you're lost in it all. My head fills with echoes of your cries and I swear I can smell you. My body contracts and I let out a howl, half joy, half anguish, and shudder into climax. Jen clamps a hand over my mouth to quiet me and I scream out the pleasure and pain into her palm.

I hardly remember what happens immediately afterward but somehow we are all dressed, a little fatigued, and splitting off in the car park. Justine is the only one who meets anyone's eye. Jen looks at her meaningfully but doesn't say a word to anyone. I leave with a nod.

Driving home, too exhausted to cry, I wonder if I will go back again. I wonder if this is healing or hurting me. You had hoped it would heal me and help me learn now that you are gone, but I don't know whether I will ever be able to make love to someone without you filling my head.

When I pull up at my drive I am so I tired I almost forget to lock the car. Dragging myself to the front door, I stop in my tracks. Sitting solemnly on the doorstep under the porch light, there you are, shivering and red-eyed. My brain fizzes when you look at me. I move to speak but you answer me with your eyes, pleading and dark and sorry.

"Is it too late?" you whisper, as I step unsteadily to the front door. I sink to my knees beside you on the step, unable to speak, and shake my head.

UNDERSKIRTS

Kirsty Logan

Girl Number One
She found me with my hands around chickens, fingers stretched
wide, thumbs over beaks. My skirt, mud weighed, tugged at my
ankles as I dipped low. Silly to curtsey while armed with birds, I
knew, but it had to be done. If I'd let go they'd've flown at her,
chuttering through her red hair. And what a sight that would've
been! The lady, still horsed, with her legs one on either side and
her skirt hitching up to show a hand-span of stocking. And her
horse as white as cuckooflowers, with its little red haunch-spot
not quite hidden by the bridle. I kept my thumbs tight over those
dangerous beaks.

So there I was, tangle skirted and chicken full, and I'll never
know what she saw in me then. Enough, any case, to offer coins
to my father—bags full of glinting, enough to make his mous-
tache disappear into the folds of his lips. For my mother, it was
the title. Lady's Maid. Fine fetters for the youngest of eight, last
to leave. No word from my siblings for years, long gone as they

were—the last we saw was the hellfire from their heels across the tops of the hills. And my betrothed, he of the thick knuckles and pale gold hair? The transparent boy who tumbled me across hay, who licked at my earlobes and stickied my palms? I forgot him within a day.

I'll never know what My Lady saw in me, but I know what I saw in her. She was a mirror. Mud weighed and bird handed as I was, she still knew me. She knew the things I had been thinking, down deep between my lacings, under the wooden heels of my shoes. The words I shaped with straw before kicking away: she knew them. We were tied as sisters, cousins, lovers. This link between us is a red silk ribbon, a fine silver chain, a length of daisies punched together. It's the loveliest thing I ever saw.

The Housekeeper
I'll not be taking part in Mistress's activities, oh no. She brings the girls up to the house and that is as it is, but I'll have none of it. She's a fancy lady, no doubt. But even fancy ladies don't need a dozen handmaids, and them changing every few weeks to a new crop of girls. It's to the end that I can't even remember their names, not a one, not a single one. Just a *you there* will suffice for that sort of girl, to my mind.

Such harlotry in their little looks! Mouths round and red like quims, and their bodices low as anything. The mistress must pick out the stitches before she gives the girls the dresses, mark you. No proper dressmaker would make a lady look such a pinchcock.

The first maid was fine enough—Mistress did need help with her dressing and suchlike, and her red cheeks and brown hair looked regular enough to fit in at the house. For a while she tied Mistress's corsets and arranged Mistress's hair, and I kept firm out of their way. Plenty to keep me busy kitchen-side. But

I couldn't pretend I didn't see what Mistress was about. Tip-tapping through the back corridors where she'd no business to be, flipping up skirts and losing her rings inside girls. Mistress parading those wagtails thinking it was like to tempt me, thinking I was like to be kept feverish at nights with thinking of their ways, that I was like to be some dirty tom. And me with my eyes on the floor like I'm meant! They'll go to the devil, the lot of them. I've got two eyes; how long can I pretend I don't see, hmm?

The Lady
Oh, how I have loved. My days are flaxen and holy with love. My nights are viscous, lucid, spilling over. My finger-pads hum. The roots of my hair feel gold-dipped; the meat of my eyes is speckled with gold; gold dust blows across my cheeks. The girls, the girls, and their love. No need for sleep when their saliva is sustenance. Their sweet country cunts and their kiss.

I find them, I whisper of my home, and they're up on my horse before the daisies close. The look in their eyes is clean as dawn. Their fingers in my mouth taste of buttermilk. My castle is a mother, is a lover. Once upon a time, I say, and they follow my hooves inside the walls, and I close the door up tight behind them.

My enchantments keep them for a turn of the sun or a phase of the moon, and then they find the chink in the walls and slip out faster than smoke. I know they look back. I see the light glint off their eyes.

Some do stay; one or two star-bellied and honey-fed girls. I tuck them under my swan-wing and tickle them close, close enough to share heat. They love love as I do. They see the straight line of my jaw along the length of their thighs and they see how it fits, the geometry of bodies. They have wondered for so long why nothing ever fits, why the knobs of their spines press hard on chair backs and why they can't lie parallel in bed, and then there I am. I know how to fill the gaps in a girl.

The Dinner Guest

She wanted us to know. She's proud of it, I'm sure. The strumpet. The slippering little...but let me tell you. You will see.

Two dozen guests for dinner and it was out with the partridge tongues and the songbird hearts in cages of ribs, along with wine sweet enough to pickle kittens. How the ladies cooed! Codswallop, I say. But the ladies like their food to sing.

Three courses in and we were a maid down. I knew because she was a comely thing, apple cheeked and apple breasted, with a glint in her eye like she well knew the parts of a man. I'd been devouring her charms between sips of the lamb-blood soup, and then—gone! For moments I frowned my way around the room, as surely even the most coddled maid would never dare abandon her post mid-meal. And then my eye's wanderings noticed how the lady of the house shifted in her seat! No soup ever caused such moans from a throat, and yet the lady was purring like a pussycat. Seated opposite the lady, I had an artist's perspective; full frontal, so to speak, perfect for observing that actress's change in expression. Shifting my feet under the table, I knew the shape of a body; even through the soles of my shoes I could feel it was that apple-rumped maid. And the lady moaned, and the lady wriggled; and all the other ladies peered into their soup and began moaning around their spoons.

Such soup, they cried! Such flavors! *Bravo*!

All the ladies were shifting and groaning, rocking in their seats like they had pigs rutting away at them. You'd have thought it was the greatest soup ever to have been swallowed.

By the bottom of their bowls, the lady was smiling wider

than a dagger's blade. The maid was back in her place, her lips plump and wet as a rose after the rain.

And so you see! That grinning tart put on quite a show for me. I know it was for me, because all that ladies do is for the eyes of gentlemen. And I do look forward to seeing more of that lady.

Girl Number Six

I stayed for a year. I was not the only one—it was three to a bed in My Lady's chamber—but still I stayed. I don't know what I was searching for. I don't know if I found it.

Living in that house was like living inside a painting—one of those lush, dark oil paintings: a still life of overripe fruit, a severed boar's head, and a cat toying with a pitted wheel of cheese. Everywhere I went, I was sure people could smell the sweet-salt fleshness on my fingers. Men in the street stopped to stare, stopped to lick their lips, though I was shoulder-to-ankle in my cloak. Her scent went that deep: right under my flesh, all the way to the marrow. For months after I left, I would still catch the breeze of her when I angled my body just the right way. There were creases and edges of me that I just could not get to, and that is where she hid: too far down to scrub out.

My parents knew, somehow. They could smell the shreds My Lady left in me. I went back to the muck of the kitchen and the heat of the stables, but there was no good to be found. Everything was overlaid and underpinned with her. My dresses would not fit: they were too tight, too low, however much fabric I added on. My scarf would not cover my hair, and tendrils slipped like spider legs to frame my cheeks. My mouth felt always swollen, always reddened.

I married—a cutout man, all hands and knees—and I stood wide-eyed as a nun in my white dress, calm as can be, like ice would stay cool in my palms. I imagined My Lady when I vowed, thought of how she would glitter and cackle to see her bedfellow in snow-colored chiffon. I thought my vows would topple her, but she clambered up on them. She strung each word and wore them as a necklace, warming them like pearls.

I never knew what hate and love meant before My Lady.

The Lord

What makes a woman is a performance of duties, and my wife has long been womanised. I saw well enough to that. From the day I flung her across my pommel to the band of gold to the hanging of the bloodied sheet to the clockwork of the household, she is a daughter of Eve through and through. Each duty is performed admirably: she whips servants with a firm wrist, she wears her dresses better than a mannequin, and she moans louder than the priciest whore. Her mask will never slip. I do not need to see her to know that.

I dress for her dinners, do I not?

I pay gold for her trousseau, do I not?

I let her take on whichever little maidens she likes, do I not?

That is what makes me a man. I do what needs to be done. I do it fast and I do it well, and no rabbit was ever safe from my arrows.

That is her desire: a man as straight and solid as a wall for her to lean on. A woman's world is the size of the distance from the bedroom to the kitchen. What is she without me? She is unmanned, an empty case. A woman is an actress, and the only thing keeping her onstage is the width of her smile.

I am born a man. I do not need to perform.

The Daughter

Yes, I told. My father deserved to know. He's a devil with a clefted chin but he still needed to know about my mother's wickedness because it was not right. It was not holy. The path to glory is not paved with swooning girls and no one ever found grace between two legs. So I told and I told and afterward I glowed for days.

God knew about my mother's sins and my father is the God within these walls so he should have known too. It was my duty, that is all, and it did not matter about my own scuttering feelings or how many times I caught the flash of bare shoulders through the keyhole because it was not about that. It was about staying good. It was about grace, and keeping my own white heels straight on the shining path to heaven. My mother's feet were no good for that path, after her grubbing in the dirt like that, ingraining those maids onto her flesh. Such things cannot be cleansed and there are no dirty feet in heaven. There is no jealousy in heaven and there was no jealousy in my heart over those girls. They were welcome to my mother. She was a pitcher full of filth with her mouth full of blood and I did not want her attention. I did not want it.

My glow was not from the deed of my telling, understand. It was from the knowledge of God, deep inside me the knowing of all His glory, His radiance warming me through the dark of night. It was grace shining out of me.

I had to do it. I had to tell, for the sake of good.

The Friend

I attended their house for dinner, the same as a dozen other lords and ladies. I expected an elegant dinner—rabbit tongues, perhaps, or eel's eyes—and wine in five different colors. The lady served all my expectations, and her conversation was characteristically delightful—all scandals and intrigues with veiled names. She laughed and touched my hand at all the right moments, and like a fool I was charmed. Me, in a gown with patched underskirts and my jewelry only paste—I was the one the lady wanted! No man ever seduced with such confidence. Her smile was as warm as fresh-baked bread, but her eyes were sharp at the corners.

I did not expect to become entangled in her activities. But I tell you; no one could have resisted the lady. After dinner the gentlemen slumped off for cigars and brandy, and the ladies fluttered to the sitting room for champagne. It was not usual for ladies to have so many drinks—it does go to one's head, and as every lady is told, there is not much in her head to absorb all that alcohol. It sloshes about in the space. That must be why I was fooled as I was—it must be!

One by one the gentlemen visited our sitting room and held out their hands for their ladies. One by one the ladies flitted out. The room was sotted with champagne and the walls were undulating—I swear they were, the lady is a magician!—and then it was just me and the lady, and then the sitting room became the lady's chambers. The girls' hands were soft as the insides of furs. Their laughter was church bells and their kisses; oh, their kisses. I had never known it could be such a way.

Our discarded skirts were piled high as a church steeple and our throats hummed with lust and we felt honey flow from our bodies and finally the lady sat at the peak of a tangle of girl-limbs and surveyed her kingdom, when in walked the Lord.

The Girls' Mothers

We knew. From the start, we knew. But we knew too what our girls were. This world is a cold and rutted place for those with brows raised above the horizon.

A handful of shiny circles and these girls are tied to any neat-shoed lady, like or not—but we liked it fine, shame to confess. We liked the words of this Lady and the promise of ever after.

The love of a mother for her child is stronger than tides, but we know that the best way for a child is to put one foot in front of the other. Half of a woman is given away each time we split ourselves with child, until all we cradle at night is a scrap of soul. The Lady was a shining road, flat and straight enough for our girls, and she would lead them into the dawn. Our girls had always had itching feet. So we took the coins and we took the promises, but they did not fill the space our girls left.

At nights we pushed with all our breath to hear the thoughts of our girls, but even the harness of daughter to mother can be severed if the walls are thick enough. The Lady's walls were thicker than muscle, and we could not break through. We made believe that our girls smiled like they always had strawberries in their cheeks, and that their shoes were silky as a pigeon's neck-feathers. We were not the stepmothers from fairy tales. We did what we thought was best.

We knew what the Lady was, but we liked her shipwreck-quick smile and the shine on her shoes. We liked her white horse with its one red spot. That horse was just like our girls, we knew, and no amount of whitewash can cover that red dot.

The Abbot

It is easy to understand why a lady would wish to escape. We all tire of this earthly plain before long. The way out is grace, and glory exists inside all of us.

The entry into heaven cannot be rushed, and for the Lady it will be as slow as she needs it to be. The duty of an anchoress is no easy one; we know that well enough. The contemplation of the grave is perhaps the most difficult, but the Lady has as much time as God has granted her. She is young yet, and there is plenty of time for her to appreciate the gifts of her enclosure. She will find peace in solitude, I am sure.

Her husband has assured me that the Lady has craved bare walls and silenced voices for many a year. The Lady is fortunate indeed that her husband is willing to sacrifice his wife for her own good. It cannot be easy for him to run a household of women alone, but he is a good man to think only of his dear wife, and I am sure that God will reward him.

The Lady's enclosure begins this evening, and I must prepare. The road to heaven is a pebbled one, and she will need a firm hand to steer her through. The contemplation of darkness will help her better than the touch of a hand ever could. Of this, I am sure.

The Lady

My skin hums with it. My flaxenbelly and my moonsmoke, and there are holes, there are holes in me through which the love escapes. The men are men and they are hard, there are no summits to them, nothing to climb up or slip down. My fingers fit into the gaps between the bricks. The moon is the size of my eye. The buttermilk and the daisies, the redness inside cheeks and within the holiest of holies, within the edges of a girl, and this is grace, and this is glory.

ABOUT THE AUTHORS

NIKKI ADAMS lives amid the quiet fields of southern New Jersey. This is her first published work of erotic fiction.

VALERIE ALEXANDER is a writer who lives in Arizona. Her work has been previously published in *Best Lesbian Erotica*, *Best of Best Women's Erotica* and other anthologies.

ZOE AMOS is the pen name Janet F. Williams uses for lesbian-themed romance, erotica and contemporary fiction. You can read her work in *Ultimate Lesbian Erotica 2006* and *2008*, and *Best Lesbian Love Stories 2010*. For more stories and nonfiction, please search for either name and please visit JanetFWilliams.com.

ANAMIKA has published three novels and a number of stories in India and abroad. *Hem and Football* and its sequel, *Hem and Maxine* dealt with women's football and lesbian love. "Ladies

Coupe" was in *Best Lesbian Erotica* 2011. Anamika lives in a satellite township near Delhi, India.

SALLY BELLEROSE is author of *The Girls Club*, which won the Bywater Prize. Bellerose's current project is a short-story collection, *Peeing Like a Boy*, which features old women behaving badly. Please visit her at sallybellerose.wordpress.com.

TENILLE BROWN's erotic fiction is widely published online and in nearly forty print anthologies including *Chocolate Flava 1* and *3*, *Curvy Girls*, *Making the Hook Up*, *Going Down*, *Best Bondage Erotica 2011* and *2012*, *Sapphic Planet* and *Suite Encounters*. The Southern wife and mother blogs at therealtenille.com.

RACHEL CHARMAN is a journalist and author from Essex, UK. Her work has also appeared in *Best Lesbian Erotica 2011* and *Ultimate Uniforms*. Contact her at ray_charman@hotmail.com.

V. C. CLARK's erotic short stories have been published on Oysters&Chocolate.com and in numerous anthologies including: *Sugar and Spice: Kinky Girl-on-Girl Stories* and *Bad Romance*. Her first novella is *The Mistress*.

ANDREA DALE would wear comfy clothes to win a contest but dresses up sexy for rock concerts. Her work appeared in the Lambda Award–winning anthology *Lesbian Cowboys: Erotic Adventures* and *Romantic Times* and *Fairy Tale Lust*, as well as about one hundred other anthologies. Visit cyvarwydd.com to find out what she's up to today.

REBECCA LYNNE FULLAN is a writer of various stripes, most of them human. She lives, writes, reads and learns in New York City. This story is for her girlfriend, Charlotte. Come visit her here: rebeccalynnefullan.wordpress.com.

PENNY GYOKERES writes poetry, music and erotic adventures, though she would like to write a full-length novel that sells triumphantly worldwide so she can retire comfortably. She was born in Toronto, Ontario, and resides there and "up north" with her partner.

SONYA HERZOG is a fortysomething, lesbian, Yankee transplant living in the deep South with her partner, son, dog and two cats. She enjoys cooking and all things literary: reading, writing and editing. She wishes there were more hours in a day to spend with friends and take up new hobbies.

KIRSTY LOGAN lives in Glasgow, Scotland with her very own fancy lady. She has published stories in *Best Lesbian Erotica 2011* and *2012,* and *Best Women's Erotica 2011.* She is working on a novel, *Rust and Stardust,* and a story collection, *The Rental Heart and Other Fairytales* (which includes "Underskirts"). Say hello at kirstylogan.com.

SID MARCH is a nomadic being with half a dozen hometowns who writes obsessively when no one is watching as a way to tame her insatiable wanderlust.

ANNA MEADOWS is a part-time executive assistant, part-time housewife. She writes from her heritage in the Mexican-American Southwest and her passion for stories about women in love. Her work appears in a number of anthologies, including fourteen from Cleis Press, and on the Lambda Literary website. She lives with her sapphic husband in California.

MAGGIE MORTON lives in Northern California with her partner and their Japanese Bobtail. Her first novel, an erotic lesbian romance, is *Dreaming of Her*. Her writing appears in multiple anthologies, and includes the lesbian erotica story "Julie Repents."

HELEN SANDLER (www.helensandler.co.uk) is about to reissue her erotic novel *Big Deal* as an e-book. She has edited Lambda-winning anthologies for Diva Books; she runs Tollington Press and co-programs L Fest. Before moving with her girlfriend to a cabin on the Welsh coast, she was a compere at London's Bar Wotever.

BD SWAIN started writing queer smut because of a deep need to do so. Read more of her writing at bdswain.com.

AMELIA THORNTON is a very good girl with very bad thoughts, who enjoys baking, hard spankings, vintage lingerie and writing beautiful naughtiness. She has been published in *Best Women's Erotica 2011* and *2012* and several Xcite anthologies, and lives by the English seaside.

With a penchant for flash fiction, **MAGGIE VENESS's** stories have been described as quirky, contemplative and mischievous. She lives on the sunny coast of northern NSW, Australia, where she tutors fiction writing at a local college and works part-time in two volunteer positions.

Jamaican-born **FIONA ZEDDE** (www.fionazedde.com) lives and writes in Tampa, Florida. She is the author of several erotic lesbian romance novels, including the Lambda Literary Award finalists *Bliss* and *Every Dark Desire*. Her novel, *Dangerous Pleasures*, was winner of the About.com Readers' Choice Award for Best Lesbian Novel/Memoir. *Nightshade*, her latest work, is available now.

ABOUT THE EDITORS

JEWELLE GOMEZ is the author of seven books including the cult favorite lesbian vampire novel, *The Gilda Stories,* winner of two Lambda Literary Awards. Her most recent play, "Waiting for Giovanni," premiered at New Conservatory Theatre Center in San Francisco in 2011. Her new novel, *Televised,* is looking for a publisher.

KATHLEEN WARNOCK is a playwright and editor. Her erotica has appeared in *Best Lesbian Erotica, A Woman's Touch, Best Lesbian Romance* and *Friction 7.* Her fiction, essays and reviews have been seen in *Love, Christopher Street; ROCK-RGRL; BUST; Ms.; Metal Maidens; It's Only Rock and Roll; Gargoyle* and the liner notes for the Joan Jett CD *Unfinished Business.* Her plays have been produced in New York, Ireland and England, and regionally in the United States. *Rock the Line* was produced by Emerging Artists Theatre in New York and won the Robert Chesley Award for Emerging Playwright. She is curator of the Robert Chesley / Jane Chambers Playwrights Project for TOSOS Theater, and Playwrights Company Manager for Emerging Artists Theatre. She is Ambassador of Love for the International Dublin Gay Theatre Festival and a member of the Dramatists Guild. She curates the Drunken! Careening! Writers! reading series at KGB Bar in NYC (since 2004). Website: kathleenwarnock.com; Twitter: @kwarnockny.

More from Kathleen Warnock

More of the Best Lesbian Erotica

Buy 4 books, Get 1 *FREE*

Sometimes She Lets Me
Best Butch/Femme Erotica
Edited by Tristan Taormino

Does the swagger of a confident butch make you swoon? Do your knees go weak when you see a femme straighten her stockings? In *Sometimes She Lets Me*, Tristan Taormino chooses her favorite butch/femme stories from the *Best Lesbian Erotica* series.
ISBN 978-1-57344-382-1 $14.95

Lesbian Lust
Erotic Stories
Edited by Sacchi Green

Lust: It's the engine that drives us wild on the way to getting us off, and lesbian lust is the heart, soul and red-hot core of this anthology.
ISBN 978-1-57344-403-3 $14.95

Girl Crush
Women's Erotic Fantasies
Edited by R. Gay

In the steamy stories of *Girl Crush,* women satisfy their curiosity about the erotic possibilities of their infatuations.
ISBN 978-1-57344-394-4 $14.95

Girl Crazy
Coming Out Erotica
Edited by Sacchi Green

These irresistible stories of first times of all kinds invite the reader to savor that delicious, dizzy feeling known as "girl crazy."
ISBN 978-1-57344-352-4 $14.95

Lesbian Cowboys
Erotic Adventures
Edited by Sacchi Green and Rakelle Valencia

With stories that are edgy as shiny spurs and tender as broken-in leather, fifteen first-rate writers share their take on an iconic fantasy.
ISBN 978-1-57344-361-6 $14.95

Best Erotica Series

"Gets racier every year."—*San Francisco Bay Guardian*

Best Women's Erotica 2012
Edited by Violet Blue
ISBN 978-1-57344-755-3 $15.95

Best Women's Erotica 2011
Edited by Violet Blue
ISBN 978-1-57344-423-1 $15.95

Best Women's Erotica 2010
Edited by Violet Blue
ISBN 978-1-57344-373-9 $15.95

Best Bondage Erotica 2012
Edited by Rachel Kramer Bussel
ISBN 978-1-57344-754-6 $15.95

Best Bondage Erotica 2011
Edited by Rachel Kramer Bussel
ISBN 978-1-57344-426-2 $15.95

Best Fetish Erotica
Edited by Cara Bruce
ISBN 978-1-57344-355-5 $15.95

Best Lesbian Erotica 2012
Edited by Kathleen Warnock. Selected and
introduced by Sinclair Sexsmith.
ISBN 978-1-57344-752-2 $15.95

Best Lesbian Erotica 2011
Edited by Kathleen Warnock.
Selected and introduced by Lea DeLaria.
ISBN 978-1-57344-425-5 $15.95

Best Lesbian Erotica 2010
Edited by Kathleen Warnock.
Selected and introduced by BETTY.
ISBN 978-1-57344-375-3 $15.95

Best Gay Erotica 2012
Edited by Richard Labonté. Selected and
introduced by Larry Duplechan.
ISBN 978-1-57344-753-9, $15.95

Best Gay Erotica 2011
Edited by Richard Labonté.
Selected and introduced by Kevin Killian.
ISBN 978-1-57344-424-8 $15.95

Best Gay Erotica 2010
Edited by Richard Labonté. Selected and
introduced by Blair Mastbaum.
ISBN 978-1-57344-374-6 $15.95

In Sleeping Beauty's Bed
Erotic Fairy Tales
By Mitzi Szereto
ISBN 978-1-57344-367-8 $16.95

Can't Help the Way That I Feel
Sultry Stories of African American Love
Edited by Lori Bryant-Woolridge
ISBN 978-1-57344-386-9 $14.95

Making the Hook-Up
Edgy Sex with Soul
Edited by Cole Riley
ISBN 978-1-57344-3838 $14.95

* Free book of equal or lesser value. Shipping and applicable sales tax extra.
Cleis Press • (800) 780-2279 • orders@cleispress.com
www.cleispress.com

More of the Best Lesbian Romance

Best Lesbian Romance 2012
Edited by Radclyffe

Best Lesbian Romance 2012 celebrates the dizzying sensation of falling in love—and the electrifying thrill of sexual passion. Romance maestra Radclyffe gathers irresistible stories of lesbians in love to awaken your desire and send your imagination soaring.
ISBN 978-1-57344-757-7 $14.95

Best Lesbian Romance 2011
Edited by Radclyffe

"*Best Lesbian Romance* series editor Radclyffe has assembled a respectable crop of 17 authors for this year's offering. The stories are diverse in tone, style and subject, each containing a satisfying, surprising twist."—*Curve*
ISBN 978-1-57344-427-9 $14.95

Best Lesbian Romance 2010
Edited by Radclyffe

Ranging from the short and ever-so-sweet to the recklessly passionate, *Best Lesbian Romance 2010* is essential reading for anyone who favors the highly imaginative, the deeply sensual, and the very loving.
ISBN 978-1-57344-376-0 $14.95

Best Lesbian Romance 2009
Edited by Radclyffe

Scale the heights of emotion and the depths of desire with this collection of the very best lesbian romance writing of the year.
ISBN 978-1-57344-333-3 $14.95

Fuel Your Fantasies

Carnal Machines
Steampunk Erotica
Edited by D. L. King

In this decadent fusing of technology and romance, outstanding contemporary erotica writers use the enthralling possibilities of the 19th-century steam age to tease and titillate.
ISBN 978-1-57344-654-9 $14.95

The Sweetest Kiss
Ravishing Vampire Erotica
Edited by D.L. King

These sanguine tales give new meaning to the term "dead sexy" and feature beautiful bloodsuckers whose desires go far beyond blood.
ISBN 978-1-57344-371-5 $15.95

The Handsome Prince
Gay Erotic Romance
Edited by Neil Plakcy

A bawdy collection of bedtime stories brimming with classic fairy tale characters, reimagined and recast for any man who has dreamt of the day his prince will come. These sexy stories fuel fantasies and remind us all of the power of true romance.
ISBN 978-1-57344-659-4 $14.95

Daughters of Darkness
Lesbian Vampire Tales
Edited by Pam Keesey

"A tribute to the sexually aggressive woman and her archetypal roles, from nurturing goddess to dangerous predator."—*The Advocate*
ISBN 978-1-57344-233-6 $14.95

Dark Angels
Lesbian Vampire Erotica
Edited by Pam Keesey

Dark Angels collects tales of lesbian vampires, the quintessential bad girls, archetypes of passion and terror. These tales of desire are so sharply erotic you'll swear you've been bitten!
ISBN 978-1-57344-252-7 $13.95

Ordering is easy! Call us toll free or fax us to place your MC/VISA order.
You can also mail the order form below with payment to:
Cleis Press, 2246 Sixth St., Berkeley, CA 94710.

ORDER FORM

QTY	TITLE	PRICE
_____	_____	_____
_____	_____	_____
_____	_____	_____
_____	_____	_____
_____	_____	_____
_____	_____	_____
_____	_____	_____
_____	_____	_____

	SUBTOTAL	_____
	SHIPPING	_____
	SALES TAX	_____
	TOTAL	_____

Add $3.95 postage/handling for the first book ordered and $1.00 for each additional book. Outside North America, please contact us for shipping rates. California residents add 8.75% sales tax. Payment in U.S. dollars only.

* Free book of equal or lesser value. Shipping and applicable sales tax extra.

Cleis Press • Phone: (800) 780-2279 • Fax: (510) 845-8001
orders@cleispress.com • www.cleispress.com
You'll find more great books on our website

Follow us on Twitter @cleispress • Friend/fan us on Facebook